PENGUIN ESS

A START IN LIFE

Anita Brookner was born in London in 1928 and, apart from several years in Paris, lived there until her death in 2016. She trained as an art historian and taught at the Courtauld Institute of Art until 1988. She is the author of twenty-four novels, many of which are available in Penguin.

Danielle Kroll graduated from Tyler School of Art and started her career in Anthropologie's art department. Her work spans across a variety of applications including stationery, ceramics, paintings and textiles. Danielle currently works out of her sunny studio in Brooklyn, NY. Her website is www.hellodaniellekroll.com

ANITA BROOKNER

A Start in Life

PENGUIN BOOKS

PENGUIN ESSENTIALS

UK | USA | Canada | Ireland | Australia
India | New Zealand | South Africa

Penguin Books is part of the Penguin Random House group of companies
whose addresses can be found at global.penguinrandomhouse.com.

First published by Jonathan Cape 1981
Published in Penguin Books 1991
This Penguin Essentials edition published 2017
001

Printed in Great Britain by Clays Ltd, St Ives plc

A CIP catalogue record for this book is available from the British Library

ISBN: 978–0–241–98149–8

www.greenpenguin.co.uk

Penguin Random House is committed to a
sustainable future for our business, our readers
and our planet. This book is made from Forest
Stewardship Council® certified paper.

To my friends of that summer

1

Dr Weiss, at forty, knew that her life had been ruined by literature.

In her thoughtful and academic way, she put it down to her faulty moral education which dictated, through the conflicting but in this one instance united agencies of her mother and father, that she ponder the careers of Anna Karenina and Emma Bovary, but that she emulate those of David Copperfield and Little Dorrit.

But really it had started much earlier than that, when, at an unremembered moment in her extreme infancy, she had fallen asleep, enraptured, as her nurse breathed the words, 'Cinderella *shall* go to the ball.'

The ball had never materialized. Literature, on the other hand, was now her stock in trade, if trade were an apt description of the exchange that ensued three times weekly in her pleasant seminar room, when students, bolder than she had ever been, wrinkled their brows as if in pain when asked to consider any writer less alienated than Camus. They were large, clear-eyed, and beautiful; their voices rang with confidence, but their translations were narrow and cautious.

Dr Weiss, who preferred men, was an authority on women. *Women in Balzac's Novels* was the title of the work which would probably do duty for the rest of her life. One volume had already been published and had met with discreet acclaim. Her publisher had lost interest in the other two volumes, being preoccupied with problems of his own. Dr Weiss invited him to dinner every six months and outlined forthcoming chapters into his unresponsive ear. Both wished that she did not feel compelled to do this. The book would, in any event, be completed, published, and moderately well reviewed.

Dr Weiss also blamed her looks on literature. She aimed, instinctively, at a slightly old-fashioned effect. Her beautiful long red hair, her one undisciplined attribute, was compressed into a classical chignon, much needed to help out with the low relief of her features. Her body was narrow, delicate, and had been found intriguing. A slighty hesitancy in her walk, which made her appear virginal, was in fact the legacy of an attack of meningitis, for which she had had to take sick leave, for the first, and, she intended, the last time in her professional life. Her appearance and character were exactly half-way between the nineteenth and twentieth centuries; she was scrupulous, passionate, thoughtful, and given to self-analysis, but her colleagues thought her merely scrupulous, noting her neatness with approval, and assuming that her absent and slightly haggard expression denoted a tricky passage in Balzac. In fact she was extreme in her expectations and although those expectations had never been fulfilled she had learnt nothing. When life was particularly uncomfortable she wished that time might be reversed and that she might fall asleep once more to the sound of the most beautiful words a little girl could hear: 'Cinderella *shall* go to the ball.'

But she was working on *Eugénie Grandet* and Balzac's unnervingly accurate assessment of Eugénie's innocent and hopeless love was making her uncomfortable, as it always did. *'Je ne suis pas assez belle pour lui.'* Why had her nurse not read her a translation of *Eugénie Grandet*? The whole of life might have been different. For moral fortitude, as Dr Weiss knew, but never told her students, was quite irrelevant in the conduct of one's life; it was better,

8

or in any event, easier, to be engaging. And attractive. Sometimes Dr Weiss perceived that her obsession with Balzac stemmed from the fact that he had revealed this knowledge to her, too late. She grieved over Eugénie, and this was the only permissible grief she allowed herself. Beyond the imposed limits it hovered, threatening, insinuating, subversive. Better to invite Ned to dinner again and tell him her theories about Eugénie's relations with her parents, whom she still blamed for the defection of Eugénie's lover. She was wrong to do so, she knew. For had not Balzac given the right explanation? *'Aussi, se dit-elle en se mirant, sans savoir encore ce qu'était l'amour: "Je suis trop laide, il ne fera pas attention à moi".'*

There is no need to hide one's inner life in an academic institution. Murderers, great criminals, should ideally be dons: plenty of time to plan the coup and no curious questions or inquisitive glances once it is done. Dr Weiss's colleagues maintained a state of perfect indifference to her past life. She was occasionally, over coffee, invited to witness a fit of silent hilarity, stimulated by an article in *History Today* or the *Modern Language Review*, but knowing this to be a solo performance she usually declined, murmuring that she would look at the paper later, even if she had read it rather recently. In this way academic anxieties were appeased. Only Tom, the porter, darting forward every morning with his meteorological information, appeared to be in touch with the outside or climatic world. Secretaries, their heads turned by the flattery of senior lecturers, drifted with eyes cast down like mermaids; librarians were usually writing a report on the last conference; students were voluble and uninterested. Dr Weiss's pale face prompted no speculations whatever.

And yet she had known great terror, great emotion. She had been loved, principally by a leading philologist at the Sorbonne, but that was not her story. Her adventure, the one that was to change her life into literature, was not the stuff of gossip. It was, in fact, the stuff of literature itself. And the curious thing was that Dr Weiss had never met anyone, man or woman, friend or colleague, who could stand literature when not on the page. Those endless serial stories that intimates recount to each other are trivial, banal, even when they deal in secrets. Who had the time to listen to a narrative that might have been composed in another dimension? So it seemed to Dr Weiss, who, silently, on certain evenings, let the dusk gather in her small sitting room, propped her head on her hand, and thought back to the play in which she had been entrusted with such an exacting part.

She remembered herself as a pale, neat child, with extraordinary hair that made her head ache. Most things cost her a great effort; even now she could recall her attempts, tongue protruding gracelessly, breath coming heavily, at trying to replace her cup in the exact depression of the saucer. Nurse had been patient but brisk; she was expected to grow up as fast as she could decently manage it, and to this end was supplied with sad but improving books. From Grimm and Hans Andersen she graduated to the works of Charles Dickens. The moral universe was unveiled. For virtue would surely triumph, patience would surely be rewarded. So eager was she to join this upward movement towards the light that she hardly noticed that her home resembled the ones she was reading about: a superficial veil of amusement over a deep well of disappointment.

It was these things because of the nature of her parents and her grandmother and because her grandmother's sad European past was a constant rebuke to her father George (born Georg) Weiss's desperately assumed English nonchalance. Mrs Weiss the elder wore black, slept in the afternoons, presided over the kitchen, cooked too heavily, and disapproved of her daughter-in-law. Disapproved of her? She hated her. But she would have hated anyone who claimed her son and usurped her suzerainty. Poor high-spirited Helen did not mind this too much; she was an actress, excellent in the madcap roles

11

for which her short red hair and entrancing smile well fitted her. She hated cooking, never put on weight, and was delighted to have her husband's domestic arrangements planned and her daughter's timetable supervised.

Mrs Weiss had brought with her from Berlin pieces of furniture of incredible magnitude in dark woods which looked as though they had absorbed the blood of horses. Wardrobes with massive doors and fretted cornices seemed to house regiments of midget Renaissance *condottieri*. Sideboards, in the Louis XIII style, fumed and contorted, with breaks and returns in their brooding silhouettes, supported épergnes, silver cake stands, entrée dishes, while cupboards opened beneath on to sauce boats, platters, and wine coolers. There was a separate press for the table linen, and green baize drawers in stumpy dressers held the knives and forks. The dining room table was always half laid, although all members of the household tended to eat separately; Mrs Weiss longed to preside over a roomful of sons and their spouses, but was forced, through the raggedness and temporary character of her translated life, to sit first with George at breakfast, then with the child and the nurse at lunch, and with the child and the nurse at tea, and at their supper. Helen came home late, when she was working, and George joined her for a snack, which felt illicit and always provoked giggles. George adored his English wife; she had all the lure of an alien species. And a forbidden one, for he had married her against his mother's wish.

To the child it seemed as if all dining rooms must be dark, as if sodden with a miasma of gravy and tears. She imagined, across the unknown land, silent grandmothers, purple flock wallpaper, thunderous seascapes, heavy meats eaten at speed. Velvet curtains, the damask cloth laid over only half the table, the intricate siege architecture of the chair legs and cross bars. Nurse cheerful, English, unimpressed by anything except the quality of the food. The doleful atmosphere at mealtimes the

12

child assumed to be universal, as if the faintly sour flavours of the buttermilk, rye bread, caraway seeds, cucumbers, had something penitential about them. She was named for her grandmother: Ruth. They got on well, each as silent as the other, brooding, obsessed with absent families, one real, the other between the covers of the same unending book. Nurse seemed an alien, a caretaker, a servant. In that dining room, while her grandmother buttered a poppy seed roll for her, the child learned an immense sense of responsibility. After the meal, while her grandmother slept in a small velvet armchair under the window, the child accepted silence as a natural condition. She disliked other children because they made such an uninhibited noise.

If the dining room belonged to her grandmother, the drawing room was Helen's. It was light and bright and frivolous, and it had a piano and a lot of photographs in silver frames and cut glass vases filled with slightly stale flowers, and a white carpet. It looked exactly like the set for one of Helen's more successful comedy roles and she used it as an extension of her dressing room; women friends dropped in on those afternoons when Helen had no matinée and they all drank tea and nibbled biscuits and smoked. There was a great deal of frail china, collected by an aunt on George's side, in cabinets: never used because Helen was careless about these things and preferred the kitchen cups. Her friends dated from before her marriage; they were actresses or singers, rather noisy, good-humoured, heavily made-up. 'Poor Helen,' they said to each other as they left the flat. 'Can you imagine living with that mother-in-law? George is a sweetie, of course, but a tiny bit dull. And the child doesn't seem too bright.' But Helen did not seem to mind. She was still beautiful and successful, her thin cheeks and jaw still unmodified by advancing years, and she was only interested in living in the present. Her quarters seemed less substantial than the grandmother's.

13

More alluring, but less safe. At any moment, the child felt, the friends might try to rescue her mother from the alien atmosphere into which she had fallen and take her away with them, back to the West End and a shared past of theatrical digs, and a late supper somewhere. They had the advanced girlishness of their profession, and they were high-spirited and petulant and charming.

There was a great deal of charm about, not only from Helen but from George or Georg himself. George as Georg obediently ate two boiled eggs under his mother's gaze every morning, retired to his dressing room and re-emerged as George, glossy and cheery, a bit of a dandy, off to Mount Street where he dealt in rare books. This profession left him a great deal of time, and as he was of a gregarious disposition he frequently attended his wife's rehearsals or dropped in to the theatre with a fresh supply of cigarettes or an invitation to lunch. If Helen was insubstantial, George, for all his wholesome presence, was more insubstantial still. Or perhaps he was simply inaccessible. With his ready smile, smart tweed suits, and heavy gold ring, George had no quarters or attributes, like the female members of the family. His shop, which the child had visited, was not even a real shop. George was affable, by nature and by profession. He was a good son, a tender father, but against these admirable sentiments, of which his mother approved, he was passionately in love with his wife. And yet he was unfaithful to her. He had an assistant, a Miss Moss, with whom he spent the evenings until it was time to collect his wife from the theatre. To Miss Moss he confessed to being unhappy, vaguely and unspecifically unhappy, a man with unrealized aspirations which he had almost forgotten. He even, to please Miss Moss, pretended to doubt his wife's fidelity. Miss Moss, who also cooked him a snack in the evenings, took him seriously and thereby proved herself invaluable. George's unhappiness stemmed largely from the fact that most of the time he did the listening. Talking was, for him, quite a thrilling experience. Miss Moss understood this; she too was a great reader and knew that there might be something in the past that made George feel unsafe. When George left, at around ten thirty, she would wash up, straighten her little flat, and retire to bed with a novel. George, refreshed, would take his bearable melancholy (for it was genuine) round to the stage door. For his wife he must be all smiles. And he was. Sitting astride a chair, joking with members of the company, he was the jovial and expansive provider. He enabled Helen to be her adorable self. As she became more girlish and outrageous, he too enacted his role, supplying her with forgotten names, lighting her cigarette, seizing her hand and kissing it, all without interrupting the babble of talk which she kept up until the excitement of the evening wore off and it was time for George to take her home.

Poor Helen. Poor George. The grandmother knew, and bore the knowledge grimly and in silence, that her son was a lightweight and her daughter-in-law a lighter weight still, that each needed the protection of the other, that neither had grown up or would be able to grow old, and that their ardent and facile love-play would damage the child. She knew that had it not been for the accident of her late husband transferring his stock of rare books from Germany to England, George would now be a car salesman or an insurance agent. He had the character for it. Helen would outlive her looks and her parts would grow smaller: her teeth were not good enough for television. The child was too quiet and too thin. Already she blinked nervously. She had no friends. None of them had friends. At this point in her reflections the grandmother would be moved to take a glass of hot milk and cinnamon to the child's bedside, persuade her to lay aside her book, and sit there until the glass was emptied and the light switched off. She retired before the silence of the dining room could be disturbed by the return of George and Helen.

The child loved her parents passionately and knew them to be unsafe. Not threatened by the dangers that had threatened her grandmother, but unsafe against disappointment. This presentiment was the strongest conviction she had. She noticed how their eyes clouded when things went wrong, how their excessive good nature could turn swiftly into argument, how little they valued her own earnest efforts. 'Darling heart,' they would call to each other, 'do come and talk to me; I'm so lonely/bored/frustrated/furious.' Their great strength, had she but known it, was that they were able to voice every passing anxiety. This process, which sounded like a litany of hardship, was in fact an alleviation of disappointment. The child registered only their disappointment, and felt apologetic about her presence which somehow marred the hectic honeymoon atmosphere which they sought to prolong. She was aware that they did no real work, that the household was supervised by her grandmother, that without her grandmother there might be no more food. She knew that her mother's bedroom was untidy, with clothes strewn about the chairs, and balls of pink-tinted cotton wool on the dressing table, that her father's dressing room contained few books but many smart clothes, that they were each separately but passionately concerned with their appearance. 'Darling heart,' called her mother, as she outlined her eyes with blue, watching her mouth uttering the words. 'Yes, darling,' called George, admiring the fit of a new jacket, tying a silk scarf at his neck. The reflections in the mirror did not suit them so well these days. Helen's teeth, George's weight were problems that would have to be faced. To the child they were still glamorous and beautiful. To the grandmother they were fools.

It was the best of times, it was the worst of times. Maintained in childhood by her youthful parents and her ageing grandmother, the girl marvelled at the stability of her world. In books, to mention only the works of

16

Charles Dickens, such great trials were undergone. Inside the flat, in Oakwood Court, there was no change. The same heavy meals were eaten at the same heavy table; the silent brooding presence of the grandmother, in her black dress, guaranteed the uninterrupted thought processes of the ruminative child. Bursts of laughter in another room signalled the presence of her parents, never to be taken for granted because of the many more attractive places they might have been. Her mother promised to buy her some pretty clothes, 'when we get to the end of this run, darling'. Her father kindly kept her supplied with books, usually in the Everyman edition, with its comfortable assurance on the fly-leaf: 'Everyman, I will go with thee, and be thy guide, In thy most need to go by thy side'. She had a room of her own, now, and did not even notice that it was as dark, as silent, as heavily furnished, as that of her grandmother. 'You'll ruin your eyes,' said Helen, 'always reading.'

But certain changes can be relied upon to take place. One hot autumn morning, the elder Mrs Weiss, placing her leather shopping bag on the kitchen table, turned a different colour, faltered, and collapsed untidily on to the floor. There was no one else in the house. When Ruth came home from school she was surprised to get no answer to her call, panicked when she entered the kitchen, and ran out to get a neighbour. The neighbour called the porter, and together they manoeuvred Mrs Weiss on to her bed. George was telephoned. Within an hour he was home, red-eyed, hapless, and smoking heavily. His first call was to a nursing agency. His second, much longer, was to the theatre. Helen was too busy to come home, and anyway she was made up for the matinée, which there was no question of cancelling. 'Just relax, darling, and don't worry. We'll get a woman in tomorrow to look after things.'

'There will be no dinner,' said George dully.

Mrs Weiss took three months to die. She lay in her

massive bed, quite unconscious, ministered to by a pair of Irish nurses who took one look at Helen and decided to do their own shopping. George rallied slightly in their company and was very gallant about offering them lifts in the car. Ruth sat with her grandmother every afternoon when she came home from school. At first she tried to talk to her, but, 'She can't hear you, dear,' said Nurse Imelda. After the first month, during which she had gazed fascinated at the heavy but childlike sleeping form and heard with dread the whistling breath, she let her attention wander. The room was stern, ancestral, but strange; she realized that she had never even seen the inside of that wardrobe. Her grandmother wore long white lawn nightdresses with drawn threadwork at the collar, slightly stained by the seepage from her mouth. After the second month, Ruth took a book in with her to the sickroom. When Mrs Weiss died, Helen was at the theatre, George was in the drawing room joking with Nurse Marie, and Ruth was reading. When Nurse Imelda, coming in to draw the curtains, said, 'I think she's gone,' she was surprised that Ruth did not lift her eyes from her book. Not until George burst in, noisily sobbing, did Ruth look up and look away. Then, said Nurse Imelda later to Nurse Marie, she did a strange thing. She took her grandmother's hand and kissed it, then raised the book to her cheek and held it there for a little while, as if for comfort. Finally she slipped out of the room and was later found in the kitchen, trying to prepare the evening meal. 'Why not?' said Helen tiredly, when she came home later, at her usual time. 'It's only until we can get a woman in. And she's bound to be better at it than I am. In the meantime, we might as well keep the nurses on for a bit. These three months have worn me out. God knows it hasn't been easy, trying to make people laugh every night, with poor Mother lying here. And you need a rest, too, darling heart. Breakfast in bed for both of us, from now on.'

18

3

So they got a woman in, Mrs Cutler, 'our darling Maggie', as Helen instantly called her, a wry, spry widow, quick to take offence. She served meals at unpunctual intervals, so that Ruth always found herself too late or too early, kept the radio on while she worked, and smoked all day. In the dining room the damask cloth was never cleared and changed only once a week; the purple velvet curtains began to smell of cigarettes; and in the sideboard cupboards the wine coolers were now gilt with tarnish. George, whose interest in the book trade had declined sharply with his mother's death, was only keeping the shop on until a suitable buyer could be found. There was no real need for him to earn money. His mother had left him some, as well as a small independent legacy to her grand-daughter, and anyway, Helen was doing well. She was making films now, comedy thrillers for which her slightly old-fashioned soubrette style was perfectly suited. So George went less to the shop and to the theatre and began to help Maggie with the shopping. They did this by car, which took a long time, longer than it had ever taken Mrs Weiss with her black leather shopping bag, but after all, they had all day. When Helen came home from the studio, she would be so tired that she would go to bed for an hour or two. At seven o'clock Maggie would take in a whisky and soda for George and a gin and tonic for Helen and herself. The ashtrays filled steadily; it was just like the old days in Helen's dressing room. Sometimes Ruth would emerge from her room, where she was doing her homework, and penetrate the smoke, interrupting her mother in the middle of an anecdote to ask if there was any supper. She was seduced and alarmed by the sight of three grown-up people behaving as if they were having a midnight feast, her mother in bed in the daytime, her father sitting astride a chair, Mrs Cutler on the edge of the bed, a cigarette in her mouth, a smear of lipstick on her chin. 'All right, Ruth, you can be heating up some soup. Just for yourself. I'll have something later. As for these two, they're well away.' They doubled up again. How delightful, how lax, how vile! So Ruth took to getting her own food, instinctively skirting the expensive made-up pies and pâtés and tinned vegetables preferred by her father and mother and above all Mrs Cutler. She made herself eggs and boiled potatoes and salads, but this spinsterish fare did not sit well on the dining room table, was not worthy of the solemn oils and her grandmother's chair, so she took to eating in the kitchen.

She did not like Mrs Cutler. She knew, without understanding, that Mrs Cutler was one of those louche women who thrive on the intimacy of couples, who are the cold-eyed recipients of many a confidence, who then repeat it to the other party in the interests of both, and whose main aim in life seems to be 'to get you two to stop making fools of yourselves and each other'. To Mrs Cutler Helen revealed many secrets of her past life without actually knowing why she did so; her training was to entertain the public, and so she supplied Mrs Cutler with the information she required, playing up to her audience like the loyal and simple actress that she was. The innocent flirtations of her youth took on a more dramatic colouring in the telling. 'That year I didn't care what I did. I thought nothing of picking up a man at a party and taking him home. And I'm not ashamed, Maggie. I sometimes wish George would have a little fling. It would make things more equal.'

'Does he still see that Miss Moss?' asked Mrs Cutler. 'Not that you've anything to worry about there.'

'Miss Moss? That woman at the shop? You can't be serious, Maggie. Throw me a ciggy, darling. I must think this over.'

Later, Mrs Cutler said to George, 'Don't you ever let me find you going off the rails again, my lad. That's a woman in a million you've got there, and I warn you, I won't be a party to any deceit.'

George laughed uneasily. He was trying to think of Mrs Cutler as his mother would have done, as a servant with an unfortunate background, but it seemed that they had slipped rather too far into intimacy for that position ever to be retrieved. And there was no doubt that she looked after Helen marvellously. It was not a bad arrangement. The flat was getting a bit shabby, but nobody was suffering. And it was good for the child to have someone constantly in the house.

The child was now fourteen and with amazed delight was mastering French. She seemed to prefer to give tongue in that language and could be heard in her bedroom chanting, *'Waterloo! Waterloo! Waterloo! morne plaine!'* The adults paused briefly while she did this. 'Not a bad delivery,' said her mother, rather surprised. 'Don't encourage her,' said Mrs Cutler. 'You know what happens to girls who get too airy-fairy. Bugger all.' They roared. Not without misgivings on George's and Helen's part, but because they thought it ungracious not to laugh at a joke. They were still eager to please, and more than ever assured of doing so.

So Ruth chanted her way through Victor Hugo until she discovered Alfred de Vigny, and then *La Maison du Berger* seemed to express her deepest thoughts. *'Pars courageusement,'* she ordered from the depths of her bedroom. *'Laisse toutes les villes.'* She even thought she might do it one day. But in the meantime she was quite happy.

21

And anyway, there was so much reading to do that she could not think of anything else. Later, perhaps.

Adolescence? It was hardly an adolescence as other girls knew it, waking up to their temporary but so exhilarating power over men. No slow smiles, no experimental flaunting, no assumed mystery for Ruth. She was in no hurry to enter the adult world, knowing in advance, and she was not wrong, that she was badly equipped for being there. In any event it seemed unattractive and nothing to do with her. Her most persistent image of the adults was that smoky bedroom, untidiness, watchfulness, and over-insistent and over-demonstrated affection. It was not unlike the world of the more advanced girls she knew, those who had changed from cheerful children into potential antagonists. Mrs Cutler's incomprehensible innuendos were all too like the clumsy sexual squibs of her contemporaries. She understood neither. She remained thin and childlike, a fact which suited Helen well enough, and badly dressed because Helen would not let her buy her own clothes and had no time to go with her to the shops. George felt a little sorry for her, sitting there in the evenings, watching television on her own, and vaguely discomfited when the voice boomed its lines of poetry from the bedroom. But George's main job in life was to keep Helen happy, a task he now performed with the aid of Mrs Cutler, who seemed to have made it her purpose in life too. Meals were now eaten from trays, the three of them cosily pigging it in the bedroom.

Ruth, except for school, was never sure where the next meal was coming from. In fact she looked on school as a sort of day nursery which could be relied upon to supply comfort in the form of baked beans and sausages, stewed prunes and custard. The work did not interest her very much for her own reading was well in advance of the syllabus. Only Miss Parker, in her pleated skirts, excited anything like interest and loyalty, but there was only one Miss Parker to go round among all the girls who had not yet set their sights on the boys wheeling round the school gates on their bicycles at four o'clock in the afternoon. Ruth was always sad when this time came. The day's security was ended, the anonymity of the school uniform no longer a guarantee, the boys on the bicycles were not for her. Sometimes she stayed on in the library, a pleasant sunny room where she was given a little job of bringing the catalogue up to date. On her library evenings she left at five, and in this way found herself at the bus stop with Miss Parker.

'What are you reading now, Ruth?' Miss Parker would say, removing the books from under Ruth's arm. 'Zola? Yes, I suppose that's no bad thing, but don't believe it all. Balzac? No, definitely not. You are much too young. Most women are too young for Balzac.'

'Tell me, Ruth,' she said, as they emerged from the bus at the other end of their journey. 'Do you understand everything you read? Does it ever worry you?'

'Yes,' said Ruth, to both questions.

As Miss Parker saw it, Ruth's only hope was to go to a university and become a scholar. It was her only hope because it was obvious that she needed to be taken into care. At fifteen, sixteen, she still dressed like a child, wore her extraordinary hair long, enjoyed her school dinner, and made her meticulous notes on the library cards. 'But I should like,' said Miss Parker to her colleague Mrs Brain, 'to subject her to an experiment. She may become a good scholar out of sheer love of the safety net beneath her. She may grow up and throw the whole thing away. Girls who are alone too much need not suffer in this day and age. They can do research. And I believe she has a little money of her own, which is no bad thing for someone without friends.'

'You'd better have a talk with the parents,' said Mrs Brain. 'Her mother's that awfully amusing actress who was always on in the West End. About five years ago now. And she read some Book at Bedtime most beautifully. Such feeling. What is she doing these days?'

Lying on her bed, Mrs Brain. Sometimes in it. Getting a little bit stiff from taking no exercise. Still apt to throw out a passionate hand to George, who is still apt to seize it and kiss it. When she had finished filming *You Must be Joking*, and no other work was immediately on offer, it seemed such a pity to break her delightful routine. Mrs Cutler, backing into the room with a tray in her arms and a cigarette in her mouth, insisted on her having a snack in bed. It was easy for George to fit in his visits to the shop around Mrs Cutler's timetable, and anyway there was a new job for him: Helen wanted to return to the stage in her own play, and he, knowing her professional strengths and weaknesses, was to encourage her to write it.

'Why not make it the story of your life?' asked Mrs Cutler, after the project had hung fire for a month or two. 'The things you've told me would fill a theatre twice nightly.'

Helen turned her still beautiful but now rather more cavernous eyes to the window and considered. 'I'm too old for the part now,' she said finally. 'But you're right, I'm sure my autobiography would sell.' She turned to George with more than enough of her old charm. 'Darling heart, buy me some nice exercise books. And a new nightie. I can work just as well in bed, better, in fact. And you can both help me. What is it, Ruth?'

'It's Miss Parker. She wants to see you and Daddy. About my going to university.'

'Who on earth is Miss Parker?'

'My form mistress. She wants you to come to the school on Friday.'

'Nonsense, darling. Invite her round for a drink if you must. But I warn you, I'm going to be very, very busy.'

For once Ruth did not leave the room. For once she

24

learned cunning. 'They all talk about you at school,' she said carefully. 'They ask me lots of questions. They still talk about you in *Lady Windermere's Fan*. And you've never been there. You or Daddy. I think you should come once. These things make a difference.' Cunning deserted her. 'And it is my future we're talking about.'

'Oh God, don't let's talk about the future. The past is so much more interesting.'

'You mean yours is,' said Mrs Cutler, who was not in the best of moods that day.

So George and Helen met Miss Parker. It was quite a while since they had been out together in the daytime and Ruth thought they were over-acting. George tucked Helen into the car as if bringing her home from hospital after childbirth. They both looked smart, anyway. It would be all right.

Miss Parker saw a rather uneasy couple. Why else should they hold hands? For protection? She noticed that they both smelled of cigarette smoke, that George's hair needed barbering, that Helen's collar had powder on it. But they were undoubtedly still attractive and seemed in no mood to disagree with her about Ruth's future.

'She's still very young for her age,' said Helen, considering her child whimsically. 'When I was her age I was very much out, I can assure you.'

'Now, now, darling heart,' replied George automatically.

They turned to Miss Parker for audience response. None came. Helen began to feel a vague but definite sense of annoyance.

'She can do whatever she likes, of course. But don't turn my baby into a blue-stocking.' She smiled her enchanting smile. 'You know how it puts men off.'

Miss Parker's determination to put Ruth into the wholesome environment of a university library at this moment received tangible shape and impetus. Whether the girl proved to be good at anything was neither here

25

nor there. Miss Parker saw, sadly, that she would become good if she had to. Ruth waited in some discomfort.

'I will coach her myself,' said Miss Parker, her colour slightly heightened. 'Her French is excellent. Good enough for the Oxford and Cambridge Boards.'

Helen rose to her feet, dropping her gloves, which Miss Parker, after a moment's hesitation, retrieved. 'We don't want her to go to Oxford and Cambridge,' she said, automatically registering her bad delivery of the line. 'We don't want to lose our baby so soon. Isn't there a university in London?'

'There are excellent French departments at several of the colleges,' said Miss Parker, with lowered eyes. 'And then, of course, she might go to France to do a little research. She needs to, well, to broaden her horizons.'

'Don't we all?' remarked Helen pleasantly and held out her hand for her gloves. 'Well, darling, that's settled. Are you pleased?'

Was she pleased? Certainly she was that evening. For Helen pronounced herself exhausted and took to her bed when she got home, just as if she had put in a day's work at the studio. George had not been to the shop at all. Mrs Cutler took in the drinks and the door closed behind her. Ruth felt restless and wandered about the flat. In Mrs Weiss's bedroom she saw Mrs Cutler's nylon peignoir on the bed, Mrs Cutler's hair rollers filling the pretty china dish with the view of the Augustusbrücke in Dresden on the dresser; on the outside of the wardrobe hangers swayed and clattered in the draught from the door and dresses slithered off them and hung precariously. There was fluff on the carpet and a stub in the ashtray by the bedside. In the dining room the original odours of meat and dumplings had long since evaporated and the air smelt stale. In the drawing room the television set, ignored because Helen did not appear on it, took up the

26

space originally occupied by Mrs Weiss's piano. In the kitchen the cold tap dripped into a coated saucepan lying in the sink.

In her room Ruth read of cottages blasted by northern winds, of country mansions with spacious lawns, of Parisian lodging houses teeming with intrigue and activity, of miners' back-to-backs vibrating with the heat of banked-up coal fires, of home farms and rectories, of villas and castles, of gardens and *pièces d'eau*, of journeys and sojourns abroad. Was real life always so untenanted? Or was real life a distillation from ordinary mundane disappointment?

As she prepared her meal the thought crossed her mind that she might one day have a home of her own. The thought did not, for some reason which she did not attempt to examine, seem overwhelmingly attractive. On further reflection she decided that she might be happier in an hotel.

4

The main advantage of being at college was that she could work in the library until nine o'clock. She thus missed the evening performance in the flat in Oakwood Court and discovered, with pleasure, that edible food was to be obtained in quite cheap restaurants. Pleasure, in fact, seemed to be on the increase. She was now able to feed and clothe herself, a fact on which she felt she ought to be congratulated, not knowing it to be quite common. She had, for the moment, no worries about money. In her own eyes she was rich, and it was known, how, she did not understand, that she was not on a grant, did not share a flat with five others, did not live in a hall of residence, and took abundant baths, hot water being the one element of life at home that Mrs Cutler could not modify.

There was also the extreme pleasure of working in a real library, with access to the stacks. What she read was perhaps less exhilarating than what she had read at school: books about books rather than the books themselves, the authors of which were always presented as the property of the various lecturers. 'Middleton? You mean the Voltaire man at Southampton?' or, 'Are you going to hear Chateaubriand today?' this last being a reference, made in all good faith, to the eminent scholar whose life's work the great wanderer turned out to be. Her only worry was to find a writer who was not already someone else's property: she did not much mind who it was.

The greed for books was still with her, although sharing them with others was not as pleasant as taking them to the table and reading through her meals. But in the library she came as close to a sense of belonging as she was ever likely to encounter. Gilded, polished, and silent, populated by noble sleepwalkers, the air quietened by a perpetual and companionable peace, whole tables set out for work, and, among the readers, an apparent cessation of vice, however temporary: these seduced her as powerfully as any more worldly scene of blandishment. Trained to keep still from earliest childhood and starved of company, she found the evening hours in the library the most satisfying of her life. When she looked up from her books, as she frequently did, it was to watch other people reading. Unaware of her gaze, they seemed innocent if a little careworn, and if they met her eye, they smiled instinctively, then dropped their eyes back to the printed page.

She read her way round and through the Romantic Movement and became quite a favourite with the Chateaubriand man; she had an extremely retentive memory and all her reciting had kept the texts well in the forefront of her mind. She was never happier than when taking notes, rather elaborate notes in different coloured ball-point pens, for the need to be doing something while reading, or with reading, was beginning to assert itself. Her essays, which she approached as many women approach a meeting with a potential lover, were well received. She was heartbroken when one came back with the words 'I cannot read your writing' on the bottom.

She bought herself a couple of pleated skirts, like those worn by Miss Parker; she bought cardigans and saddle shoes and thus found a style to which she would adhere for the rest of her life. She did not ask Helen's advice, knowing that it would not do, but enjoyed showing her the clothes. Helen thought them dreary. 'Strange that you should have turned out so different from me,' she sighed, holding out a thin nude arm with silver bracelets clashing and sliding up and down. Helen's skin was poreless, but losing its fat; she was alternately wistful and bad-tempered and tended to spurn food. George, on the other hand, was growing increasingly heavy. He was liable to wax sentimental over his daughter's apparent maturity, not recognizing it for the makeshift it was. Ruth avoided sentiment for she had seen how easy it was to come by.

The days were not long enough. Helen had decided that Ruth should pay rent for her room at Oakwood Court; this suited them both, putting a decent distance between the past and present tenancies. Ruth rose early, went out for a newspaper and some rolls, made coffee, and washed up, all before anybody was stirring. She was the neatest person in the house. As she opened the front door to leave, she could hear the others greeting the day from their beds with a variety of complaining noises, and escaped quickly before their blurred faces and slippered feet could spoil her morning. She was at one with the commuters at the bus stop, respectably accoutred for a day in public. There would be lectures until lunchtime, tutorials in the afternoon. In the Common Room there was an electric kettle and she took to supplying the milk and sugar. It was more of a home than home had been for a very long time. There was always someone to talk to after the seminar, and she would take a walk in the evening streets before sitting down for her meal in a sandwich bar at about six thirty. Then there was work in the library until nine, and she would reach home at about ten, by which time George and Helen would have taken their sleeping pills and Mrs Cutler would be safely corralled in the drawing room watching television in a cloud of smoke. It was a bit lonely sometimes, but it was better than it might have been.

'But don't you ever go out?' asked her friend Anthea. For she was surprised to find that she made friends quite easily. She was of that placid appearance and benign or perhaps indifferent disposition that invites confidences, particularly from those too restless to harbour information. In many ways Anthea was like Helen: amusing, sharp-witted, lightweight and beautiful. Needing a foil or acolyte for her flirtatious popularity, she had found her way to Ruth unerringly; Ruth, needing the social protection of a glamorous friend, was grateful. Both were satisfied with the friendship although each was secretly bored by the other. Anthea's conversation consisted either of triumphant reminiscences – how she had spurned this one, accepted that one, how she had got the last pair of boots in Harrods' sale, how she had shed five pounds in a fortnight – or recommendations beginning 'Why don't you?' Why don't you get rid of those ghastly skirts and buy yourself some trousers? You're thin enough to wear them. Why don't you have your hair properly cut? Why don't you find a flat of your own? You can't stay at home all your life. Why don't you stop skulking in here and come to the refectory? It's much livelier down there. Why don't you come to the pub with Brian and me? Why don't you have a go at Crawford? He's your type, always reading, and even if he weren't you need about fifty years' practice to bring yourself up to date.

These questions would be followed rapidly by variants beginning 'Why haven't you?' Found a flat, had your hair cut, bought some trousers. It was as if her exigent temperament required immediate results. Her insistent yet curiously uneasy physical presence inspired conflicting feelings in Ruth, who was not used to the idea that friends do not always please. She sat patiently through Anthea's dramatic reminiscences, knowing her to be on an even keel when she was on this territory. She, on the other hand, became alarmed by the too physical manifestations of Anthea's volatile temperament: the giddiness, the headaches, the sudden drenching blushes. She

31

became aware, through Anthea, that she had an extreme horror of physical illness, a loathing for which she tried to compensate by urging the other to be stronger, or calmer, or, as a last resort, more self-indulgent. It was a bad stratagem, but it worked. In the presence of the quieter girl, clearly no rival, Anthea's magnificent self-confidence revived and flourished. Ruth, concerned with her friend's aggressive charm and repressed misgivings, felt protective, for she had absorbed, at an early age, the occasional lost look in her parents' glances and was able to summon up a sturdiness she did not know she possessed in order to reassure them. This she did with Anthea, although she never quite understood why she had to, for Anthea seemed to her in every way superior.

Anthea had already run through the entire gamut of adult female experience, from promiscuity to dyed blonde streaks in the hair. She radiated sexual energy, had an eternal, almost professional, smile on her beautiful mouth, and turned her intense charm on man and woman alike. Ruth perceived only her desire to win people over. She had discovered that Anthea's mother was dead, and that she was passionately attached to her father. She lived with her lover, Brian, a quiet, almost torpid, but powerfully built physicist. It was rumoured that she was to be married to him but Ruth sensed that she was frightened to commit herself and to leave her reassuring circus of conquests. Anthea occasionally referred to this difficulty, but never discussed it openly; after betraying her anxieties she was more imperious than ever. Why don't you stop messing about with those notes and make us a cup of coffee?

Ruth abandoned caution and invited her home to tea, since Anthea's concern with her looks extended to an appreciation of those of other, better-known women. Helen had been urged to array herself for the occasion and had chosen a caftan, gold earrings and a great deal of scent. George, who had accepted an offer for the shop and was waiting for the contracts to be exchanged, was home most of the time now, and promised to collect a cake from Fortnum's. The tea was ready half an hour before Anthea arrived and Helen regally drank two cups. 'If your friend can't be bothered to turn up on time, I'm sure I can't be bothered to wait for her. Don't worry; I shall say nothing. What I can't appreciate I ignore.'

Yet the two got on famously. Ruth had not seen her mother so animated for over a year, and Mrs Cutler, returning from a visit to the chiropodist, could hear trills of laughter from the front door. Ruth and George looked on as spectators, beaming with the success of their efforts, content to act as foil for the two protagonists. Mrs Cutler had taken one look at the intent gathering and retired in disgust to her room. With that acute sense of timing that distinguishes the accomplished woman from the mere amateur, Helen and Anthea rose to say goodbye before the jokes became too prolonged and the laughter too disturbing. Ruth and her father were taken a little by surprise. 'Don't go,' said George, 'you've eaten nothing. I can easily make some more tea.'

Anthea smiled brilliantly and pressed his hand. She kissed Helen and promised to return. Ruth saw her to the door.

'And how often is that little act put on?' asked Anthea. 'I can see why you don't bring too many people home.' Anthea knew everything. 'The best thing for you to do is to find somewhere of your own. And don't leave it too late.'

'What a delightful girl,' said George, when Ruth returned to the drawing room.

'Quite pretty,' said Helen, blowing smoke down her chiselled nostrils, 'but not your type, darling. She has the soul of an air hostess.'

By the end of her second year a restlessness came over Ruth, impelling her to spend most of the day walking.

The work seemed to her too easy and she had already chosen the subject for her dissertation: 'Vice and Virtue in Balzac's Novels'. Balzac teaches the supreme effectiveness of bad behaviour, a matter which Ruth was beginning to perceive. The evenings in the library now oppressed her: she longed to break the silence. She seemed to have been eating the same food, tracing the same steps for far too long. And she was lonely. Anthea, formally engaged to Brian, no longer needed her company. Why don't you do your postgraduate work in America? I can't see any future for you here, apart from the one you can see yourself. At home, things had become a little disquieting. Helen was out of work. At least, she had chosen to be. She had been offered a couple of parts as the heroine's mother and these she had spurned with hauteur. She rarely got dressed these days, preferring to lie on her bed in the caftan and her bracelets, smoking and drinking cups of instant coffee brought in by Mrs Cutler. Like early theologians or doctors of the church, the two women would debate whether she should include this or that skirmish with a director, this or that love affair, in her autobiography. This now filled half of one of the notebooks that George had bought her two years before. As neither Helen nor Mrs Cutler possessed any literary gifts or were given to reading anything more serious than historical romances (though Helen still kept her old copy of *Anna Karenina* on the bedside table) the writing did not proceed. But points of content were hotly argued.

'If only Ruth would give me a hand,' moaned Helen.

'I don't know why you don't dictate the whole thing and let her put it together,' said Mrs Cutler.

George did not feel happy. The presence of the two women in the bedroom and, in the evening, their repetitive arguing of the same points, seemed to make him superfluous. The shop had been sold to a Mrs Jacobs, a sad-eyed widow whose husband had been in the trade and whose psychiatrist had urged her to do something useful with her time. George rather liked her, and spent some days going over the stock with her. She was grateful, but could not refrain from telling him that he had been undercharging for years and that he could have got more for the business had he tried. Miss Moss listened resentfully from the back room. George wondered, with a slight qualm, what his father would have made of the sale. He even wondered if he had been wise to sell at all, for with Helen not working and Mrs Cutler's wages to pay, the money would not last all that long. He banished these thoughts to the back of his mind and promised Mrs Jacobs that he would look in from time to time to see how she was getting on.

Even this was not so simple. With his daughter out all day, and his wife and housekeeper discussing which photographs did Helen most justice, which quotes from her album of press cuttings should be included, and from there sinking to a delightful and endless conversation about their childhoods ('Of course, I was spoiled, and once you are you never get over it, do you?' 'That was my trouble. I never cleaned the bath out until I was married. Didn't know you had to.'), George found himself doing the bulk of the dusting these days and most of the shopping as well. He was fatter and not so cheery. Sometimes he shaved only if he were going out. Helen, in her middle age, which she hated, had turned away from him slightly, as if blaming him for her advancing years. Why not? She blamed him for his own. Only Mrs Cutler, her eyes watchful, her thin frame thriving on their diet of made-up dishes and instant coffee, remained the same.

Helen was changed. She was as beautiful as she had ever been, for thin women retain their shape. But they lose what little flesh they had as time goes on. Helen was very thin. Her long narrow hands and feet, emerging from the caftan, seemed to have assumed their ultimate skeletal shape. The bones of her shoulders were sharply outlined. Her wedding ring was loose and sometimes she took it off. Her red hair was now a secret between herself and her hairdresser, and on the days when she was due to have it done she found the atmosphere in the streets threatening. Eventually, Mrs Cutler, the Hoover abandoned in the middle of the floor, would take her, leaving George to finish whatever work she had or had not been doing. On their return, both women would pronounce themselves exhausted, and Helen would retire to bed, where she knew she looked her best. George, harassed, would join her for a drink. Helen's blue eyes, more prominent now in their pronounced sockets, would gaze out of the window with a wistful and ardent expression, her thoughts winging to past triumphs, past travels, past love affairs. George, looking at her in these unguarded moments, would be shocked to see how quickly she had aged.

5

Ruth took some of Anthea's advice, had her hair cut, won a scholarship from the British Council which entitled her to a year in France working on her thesis, and fell in love. Only the last fact mattered to her, although she would anxiously examine her hair to see if it made her look any better. *'Je ne suis pas assez belle pour lui.'* Had she but known it, her looks were beside the point; she was attractive enough for a clever woman, but it was principally as a clever woman that she was attractive. She remained in ignorance of this, for she believed herself to be dim and unworldly and had frequently been warned by Anthea to be on her guard. 'Sometimes I wonder if you're all there,' said Anthea, striking her own brow in disbelief.

She did this when Ruth confessed that she was in love with Richard Hirst, who had stopped her in the corridor to congratulate her on winning the scholarship and had insisted on taking her down to the refectory for lunch. Anthea's gesture was prompted by the fact that Richard was a prize beyond the expectations of most women and certainly beyond those of Ruth. He was one of those exceptionally beautiful men whose violent presence makes other men, however superior, look makeshift. Richard was famous on at least three counts. He had the unblemished blond good looks of his Scandinavian mother; he was a resolute Christian; and he had an ulcer. Women who had had no success with him assumed that the ulcer was a result of the Christianity, or indeed the way he professed it, for Richard, a psychologist by training, was a student counsellor, and would devote three days a week to answering the telephone and persuading anxious undergraduates that it was all right to enjoy sex with every partner, or alternatively, that it didn't matter if you didn't. Then Richard would wing home to his parish and stay up for two whole nights answering the telephone to teenage dropouts, battered wives, recidivists, and alcoholics. There seemed to be no end to the amount of bad news he could absorb.

A man who did things! Her father, as far as she could see, did nothing but listen to her mother. But Richard had been known to race off on his bicycle to the scene of a domestic drama and there wrestle with the conscience of an abusive husband, wife, mother, father, brother, sister, or lover. (He had indeed let it be known that he did this.) His flat was permanently occupied by teenagers found huddled on benches at Waterloo Station, whom he took in until they either found work or escaped while he was at a lecture. The porter at the college was only too well acquainted with the distraught and usually drunk woman who appeared regularly to ask Richard to sort out an article which would redeem her whole life if published in *New Psychology*. He was rarely at home. He rarely slept. He never seemed to eat. His ulcer was the concern of every woman he had ever met in his adult life, and many were eager to tempt his palate with special bland dishes: no obligations entailed. Many were disappointed. His diet was a matter of speculation, as was his physique, which remained oddly splendid. His dark golden hair streamed and his dark blue eyes were clear and obdurate as he pedalled off to the next crisis.

Into Ruth's dazed and grateful ear he spoke deprecatingly of his anorexic girls, his unmarried mothers, and his battered wives. She thought him exemplary and regretted having no good works to report back. The race

38

for virtue, which she had always read about, was on.

'He's sick,' said Anthea, who had not taken the news of Ruth's attachment too well. 'He can't have enough of other people's problems. He's insatiable. He doesn't recognize anybody's needs, only their demands. And he glories in it. It gives him the right to be more tired, more busy, more overworked than anyone he knows. Don't expect him to be any good in bed,' she added, seeing Ruth becoming more resolute by the minute.

Ruth had no expectations of this kind. But it did cross her mind that she might invite Richard for a meal. She contemplated the dining room at home. So sad. The velvet cloth and curtains dusty and bald in patches, a pervasive, not unpleasant smell, as if some wine had gone rancid in the bottom of a neglected bottle, the handle of a china soup tureen broken off and waiting on a small silver tray to be riveted. And anyway, was it not rather old-fashioned? The kitchen yielded little more to her increasingly worried inspection. Mrs Cutler, who only washed up once a day, was in favour of letting things soak in murky water. Tins of soup and packets of cereal made up the contents of the store cupboard; the refrigerator contained a plateful of sardines, some tomatoes, many pints of milk with the cream poured off, and a jar of chicken *en gelée*. The teapot had not been emptied. In the dull evening light of a cold spring, it did not look promising. Whatever life there was left in Oakwood Court was lived on the periphery; the main rooms no longer had any function.

So Ruth took more of Anthea's advice and found a flat for herself (and for Richard or at least his dinner) in Edith Grove, a dusty but not unpleasant thoroughfare near the World's End, reverberant with heavy traffic. She had the attic floor of a large house that shuddered with every passing lorry. And although she did not know it, thinking her new home flimsy and temporary in comparison

39

with what she had left behind, she had done very well, for her two rooms, despite their low ceilings, were light and might eventually be sunny, and the large overstuffed sofa and the small narrow bed, though shabby, were clean. The other tenants of the house were two elderly ladies, Miss Howe and Miss Mackendrick. Miss Howe, who made shirts for an expensive shop in Jermyn Street, was fierce and argumentative but worked so hard at her sewing machine that these qualities were not too much in evidence. Miss Mackendrick was as tiny and thin as a child; she was sweet and vague and did nothing except tend her many plants. Ruth would look up from the street and see her in the window, her cat held lovingly to her cheek. 'Come on, Cissie,' Miss Howe would shout up the stairs. 'We're going out. Kensington High Street. Do you good.' Miss Mackendrick would whimper a protest and sometimes even shed a tear. But Miss Howe always won, and when they got back, both ladies, tired and argumentative, but feeling braver than when they had left the house, went to bed very early.

It was a most respectable house. The landlord, an elderly young man who worked at the Home Office, would look in once a month, at Miss Howe's insistence, to mark their rent books. 'He's liable for the Tribunal if he don't,' said Miss Howe inaccurately; she sometimes regretted that she had so little to complain about. The landlord, who owned two properties in Edith Grove, was abstracted but well-meaning, and regularly forced himself to drink a cup of tea in Miss Mackendrick's densely furnished and hermetically sealed rooms. Since he did without the larger income that he might have obtained by letting his house more profitably, he cut down on expenses. Ruth's water heater behaved erratically and her oven was a yawning cavern of rusting equipment. On wings of love, she cleaned and polished everything. Had she but known it, she was a desirable tenant. 'If you'd like to leave me your keys one weekend,' said the landlord, 'my wife will come in and repaper your bedroom.'

It was not a bad life in Edith Grove. Throughout that vaporous and humid early summer Ruth watched the dusty trees from her bedroom window and read cookery books to find the perfect meal for Richard's ulcer. The fact that she did so little cooking these days, and indeed had never done much at all, did not bother her. If it were a question of reading, she could do it.

She knew her parents did not miss her, but the news that she was leaving home had prompted them to an expression of intense dismay. Helen recovered much of her histrionic brilliance when contemplating this betrayal, tragically, from her bed. 'But *why* do you want to go?' she repeated. There was no logical answer. 'Only one reason, if you ask me,' said Mrs Cutler, grimly swiping at the dust on the bedside table.

'But I'll come home at the weekends,' protested Ruth. 'And I'm out all day anyway. It's not as if you see anything of me.'

'But the *nights*, Ruth, the *nights*! Supposing Daddy or I were taken ill? You can't ask Maggie to bear the whole burden.'

'Indeed you can't,' agreed Mrs Cutler.

George was more sympathetic. He went to Edith Grove, puffing up the stairs in his sharply waisted overcoat, which was now rather too tight for him. He sat on the clean shabby sofa and asked his daughter to make him a cup of coffee. Ruth served it with care. She takes after Mamma, George thought with surprise; it had never struck him before. Ruth introduced him to Miss Howe and Miss Mackendrick. George passed the test. Before he left, he telephoned Helen to say that he would soon be home. Ruth noticed a slight blankness invade his features as he received the usual list of things she wanted done. None of these was excessive but each took a long time to describe. 'And Maggie needs a new library book,'

Ruth could hear her mother saying. 'Nothing with an unhappy ending. And nothing set in the colonies. And preferably with nobody called Douglas in it.' Mrs Cutler's husband had been called Douglas.

'Daddy, I don't like Mrs Cutler,' said Ruth.

George drained the last drops of coffee from his cup. 'Never cared for her too much myself,' he replied. 'But she keeps your mother happy.'

The next evening Ruth, at her window, saw his car draw up. She went downstairs to let him in and found him on the steps holding a carton filled with damask napkins, entrée dishes, serving plates, a ladle, and some knife rests.

'Mamma would have liked you to have them,' he said.

6

'Mrs Cutler,' asked Ruth, who refused to call her Maggie, 'how do you make a chicken casserole?'

Mrs Cutler removed her cigarette from her mouth, tipping the ash into the saucer of the cup of tea she was drinking at the kitchen table.

'For how many?'

'Two.'

'I get it. Well, you can buy some chicken pieces at Sainsbury's, put them in a Pyrex dish with a tin of Campbell's mushroom soup, and bung the whole thing in the oven for a couple of hours. Dead easy. I usually serve it with a bit of rice and some frozen beans. Then you could buy one of their apple pies and warm it up for pudding.'

For once Ruth had the feeling that Mrs Cutler was doing her best. Unfortunately, it was not good enough.

'Anthea,' she asked on the following morning. 'How do you make a chicken casserole?'

'Are you still trying to get that nut to come to dinner?' Anthea carefully replenished her lipstick and smiled brilliantly at herself in her mirror. 'Why chicken casserole? Why don't you just grill him a bit of sole? You can do it at the last minute. He's been known to turn up late, you know.'

But the weather had become hot and thundery and Ruth did not trust the refrigerator at Edith Grove to préserve anything for longer than half an hour. It would have to be a chicken casserole because the oven, also slightly defective, could be relied upon to cook it very slowly. Ruth saw herself, in a long skirt and her Victorian blouse and cameo, casually taking the complete dish from the oven when Richard arrived. Besides, it would smell better.

So it would have to be the *Larousse gastronomique* in the public library.

She was appalled by the number of ingredients required and also by the fact that leeks, which figured largely in the recipe, were in short supply. She should have done all this two months ago. Eventually she located some in Harrods, poor shabby things propped up like invalids in their wooden boxes, and anxiously swathed in blue tissue paper. She bought ten, together with two melons (in case one was unsatisfactory); then, with an obscure feeling of giving in to bad advice, she bought an apple pie – rather superior, very expensive, with an overlay of lyrically golden varnish – in the bakery department. She took a taxi back to Edith Grove, put the cake in the refrigerator, the melons on the windowsill, the leeks on the table, cutting away the yellowing green parts which she took down to the dustbin as she went out with her shopping bag for the second time. On this trip she bought three pounds of new potatoes, some carrots, onions, cream, and a bottle of wine. When she got back up the stairs, she was just in time to seize her notes but not in time to catch the bus to her lecture. It would have to be another taxi.

'You all right, Miss Whatsaname?' asked Miss Howe, emerging from her basement. 'I keep hearing the door go.'

'Yes, I'm fine, Miss Howe. Just a bit late this morning.'

'All right for some,' said Miss Howe to her cat, but loud enough for Ruth to hear.

The lecture was important; Ruth heard about one

word in three. 'And so, ladies and gentlemen, in *La Cousine Bette* we have the plain woman's revenge, but Balzac has given this particular plain woman manipulative powers that most plain women cannot use. Here we have the clearest example of Balzac's own desire to manipulate his characters.' She heard that bit and nodded her head in agreement, then stopped abruptly as she realized that she had forgotten to buy another bottle of wine for the sauce. Why did simple meals cost so much, not only in terms of money but in sheer attention? One part of her would have been happier with *La Cousine Bette*, but she dismissed this as faint-heartedness. Balzac would always be there. Richard, she knew, would not.

'I shan't see you until Wednesday,' she told Anthea. 'I'm not coming in tomorrow.'

'He's not coming for the whole day, is he? You'd do better to leave everything until the last moment. What are you going to wear?'

'That blouse of my grandmother's and my tapestry skirt.'

'Not bad. Too elaborate, of course. You'll look as if you're dressing up for him.'

'Well, I am,' said Ruth humbly.

'For God's sake,' cried Anthea in exasperation. 'Why do you have to let everything show?'

At least, Ruth consoled herself, I have no manipulative powers. These, she knew, constituted the quality that distinguished the villains from the virtuous. Yet why, she thought, did Balzac take such a delight in Bette's terrible stratagems? She decided to postpone thinking about this until she had more time.

Richard was due at eight o'clock on Tuesday evening. Ruth woke at her habitual early hour of six and wondered how she was going to fill the day. With anticipation, naturally. That is how most women in love fill their day. Frequently the event anticipated turns out to be quite dull compared with the mood that preceded it. The onus for redeeming the situation rests on the other person who is, of course, in no position to know of the preceding mood. Thus both fail and both are disappointed.

In the morning, which was bright but charged with steamy cloud, she went for a walk in the cemetery to calm her mind. For a little while it worked. There was no one there but the gardener and an old man with a young child: they took small steps, their heads down, all the time in the world to spare. A rank growth of a loose purple flowering weed flowed over the graves, binding them together in a common fate. It seemed hard on the newly dead not to be able to join the others beneath the flourishing undergrowth. Vaguely deterred by the absence of a religious edifice, which would somehow give the whole excursion a weight which it presently lacked, Ruth turned homewards at half past ten and made herself a cup of coffee. The rest of the morning could be taken up with deciding where to buy the chicken. And perhaps a bunch of flowers.

She got out her notes on Racine and contemplated the plight of the stricken (but ageing) Phèdre. '*Oui, prince, je languis, je brûle pour Thésée.*' Professor Wyatt would read out that verse with a telling pause before the last two words, thus revealing Phèdre's substitution of her husband's name for that of the young man, Hippolyte, for whom she burns and languishes. Hippolyte, whose mind is occupied by 'la jeune Aricie', a suitable virgin of good family, is devoured by a sea monster as he rushes along the shore in his chariot. Richard on his bicycle, thought Ruth, although she always envisaged the episode as one of those monumental and frightening beach scenes by Picasso, showing mammoth figures with inflated arms bowling slowly along a strip of sand: a sense of nightmare behind the comedy. She did not really care for Hippolyte, she decided, although Phèdre was enough to put anyone off. The combination of outraged and thwarted sensuality and priggish inviolability (Hippolyte is a ward of the goddess Diana) seemed to her avoidable, given a little goodwill on both sides. 'As you grow older, you will come to see this as a paradigm of middle-aged love,' said Professor Wyatt. 'All you have to decide at the moment is whether the vengeance wrought is brought about by the old gods of antiquity or the new and punitive God of the Jansenists.' This was what she now tried to do.

But she was restless. And even rather unhappy. The break in her routine, occasioned by her extreme dedication to the idea of the god-like Richard was, she knew, wrong, not sensible, doomed, in fact. But it was appropriate that she should spend the day alone for the very strength of her feelings had already removed her from normal contact, and certainly from normal conversation. But how very sad it was to be alone with these feelings, when, in ideal circumstances, she might be motivated to share them.

On an impulse she telephoned her mother. Helen was having one of her better days. 'Just a minute, darling, while I drink this coffee that Maggie's just brought me.' Ruth waited while she drank the coffee, hearing it, seeing it, knowing that her mother would expect a respectful pause while this bit of business was given its full importance. Helen always had an audience, if only in her mind's eye. 'Now, my darling, why aren't you at a lecture or something?'

'I'm having this friend to dinner tonight. I thought there'd be a lot to do.'

'Well, if you've got time, darling heart, there's plenty to do here. Daddy's gone to Mount Street and Maggie's got a shopping list as long as your arm.'

'I thought Daddy had sold the shop.'

'He has, but that silly woman can't manage on her own, it seems. She pays him some sort of retainer to advise her.'

(This was quite untrue. Calling in one day out of sheer boredom, George had found Mrs Jacobs in the back room of the shop, sitting down to a simple meal of rye bread and liver sausage, with a dill pickle on the side, and a glass of lemon tea. '*Mahlzeit*,' he said automatically. He had not used the word for years. Her face brightened. 'I've brought far too much,' she confessed. 'I don't eat a lot these days. Won't you join me?' So he did and took to dropping in at the shop quite regularly after that. 'Call me Sally,' said Mrs Jacobs. 'I was named Sarah, of course. After my mother.' They became Sally and George quite easily. Miss Moss handed in her resignation.)

While George, waited upon once again, sipped his lemon tea in Mount Street, Ruth and her mother and Mrs Cutler sat down to tinned tomato soup, cheese on toast, and instant coffee at Oakwood Court. The aromatic plates were slipped casually into a brimming washing-up bowl by Mrs Cutler and left there to soak. The two women lit cigarettes with an air of exhaustion. Ruth felt a sudden surge of affection for them, Helen in her caftan and bracelets, Mrs Cutler in her dress uniform of elephant-coloured trousers, nylon blouse, and remedial footwear. They managed to be so busy doing the little they had to do. They carried their packets of cigarettes around with them like talismans; they called for cups of coffee; Helen refurbished her make-up with severe and practised strokes; even when they took a rest in the afternoon they made it sound like an assignment to be fitted into a busy day. And then there would be tea – they both groaned for it – and then George would be home, more cheerful than of late, bearing something expensive to eat, and then they would all spruce themselves up for drinks at six. At eight o'clock they would start groaning again, exhausted by their day; Maggie would make a few sandwiches and take them in on a tray; they would swallow a last drink, take their sleeping pills and retire to bed.

Mrs Cutler would change into her slippers and dressing gown and watch television until it closed down for the night.

Ruth, in her neatness, admired the agreeable air of lavishness and laissez-faire that reigned at Oakwood Court. It was as if they had all come down in the world and were determined to let everyone know it. They must spend as much on drink as on food, thought Ruth, but they seem to flourish on it. My mother always seems clean and scented, although slightly dusty, somehow. She doesn't go out enough, of course. But really, when you come to think of it, they aren't having too bad a time. There was no need to worry about them. And they seemed to keep themselves amused.

'How's the writing?' she asked.

Helen, clenching and unclenching her jaw muscles to keep them firm, could not reply.

'I think I might try a short story,' she said eventually. 'The television people would have it. I have this knack for dramatic situations, and I might even write in a part for myself. I've been away too long.'

'Mother,' said Ruth suddenly and urgently. 'There's this man coming to dinner tonight and I'm terrified.'

Helen's blue eyes turned clouded and vague. She was silent and seemed remote, vaguely offended. But all she said was, 'I won't tell your father. He is so frantically anxious in case you do something unsuitable. He'd have kept you at home, if at all possible. No, say nothing. Terrified?' She gave a very small smile. 'There's no need to be. No need at all.'

7

She returned home in the early afternoon, with her
chicken, and wondered what to do next. By then she was
dreamily depressed, half longing for the day to be over.
She had not known that a state of waiting could be so
consuming an affair. The flat was clean; the sun, now hot
and strong, lay in a shaft over the window seat and along
the old flowered carpet. Through the window she could
see lorries loading and unloading in the depository. Miss
Howe and Miss Mackendrick must have gone on one of
their expeditions, for there was no noise or movement
in the house. She sat in the shaft of sunlight and reflected
how little there was to do when she was not working.
She could not even settle to a book. In any event, she had
been reading less since her first meeting with Richard.

At four o'clock she made a cup of tea and carried it
back to her shaft of sunlight, as if seeking protection. She
wished she had stayed on at Oakwood Court to see her
father but it would have been too much of a rush to get
back and she was afraid that all the shops would suddenly
run out of chicken. Half reluctantly she made some sort
of timetable: the preparation of the meal, the bath, the
insertion of the dish into the oven, dressing, and then
what Mrs Cutler called the finishing touches.

She had no confidence in any of it any more, and she
knew that food, however mediocre, must be served with
authority. Timing the rice was going to be particularly
tricky. If Richard was due at eight, she should put the

water on to boil at seven thirty. She had not given this problem due consideration; it almost annoyed her to have to give it her consideration now. Problems to which there is no solution waste a lot of one's time, she reflected.

She became alarmed at her dispirited condition, picked up Balzac's *Un Début dans la Vie*, got annoyed by the excessive geographical information given in the first few pages, realized that she would have to travel fairly widely in the provinces when she got to France, and became slightly cheered by this faint indication that life might hold some substance beyond the events of this particular evening. Here she reached the heart of her curious distress, for if this evening did not turn out well, did not produce some indication of future progress, did not in fact elicit some sort of plan from Richard, she was devoid of resource for making anything happen to them both in the future. She really did not see that she could take days off and spend her life perusing the *Larousse gastronomique* in the event of being able to proffer another, identical, invitation. She did not realize that most men accept invitations to dinner simply in order to know where the next meal is coming from. Her father, who could have told her this, did not.

At five o'clock she washed up her cup and saucer, and started peeling vegetables. She sliced them and put them into cold water to soak. At five thirty she took them out of the water, browned the chicken in butter and olive oil, and arranged the vegetables in the bottom of a casserole with the jointed chicken on top. She tipped the wine into the casserole. It was ten minutes to six. Mrs Cutler had said a couple of hours. Bored with waiting, she put the dish in the oven and restored the kitchen to its former order.

She stayed as long as possible in the bath, then sprayed herself with a great deal of scent, brushed her hair for a very long time, and made up her face carefully. She was

51

in a sudden hurry to change from her weary daytime self to the more heightened self she would be that evening. Her heart had started to beat rather rapidly, and the colour was coming to her cheeks. She dressed her hair, and put on her grandmother's high-necked blouse and the tapestry skirt that showed off her slight figure. Pinning the cameo at her throat, she noted with approval that she was looking her best. It was twenty minutes to seven.

This, now, was the best of it. Waiting had become something to enjoy, to savour; waiting was almost a tribute she owed herself. The sun blazed strongly on the carpet, its shaft now pointing into a corner of the room; soon it would disappear and the curious white light of a June evening in Edith Grove would make lamps superfluous. The street noises diminished in volume as the evening rush subsided, but a sudden gust of sound, as the front door opened and closed, told her that Miss Howe and Miss Mackendrick were back. There was an agitation on the stairs: Miss Mackendrick was overtired and fretful and inclined to blame Miss Howe for the long wait at the bus stop. 'We could have gone in the Gunter and sat down if you hadn't acted so daft,' said Miss Howe scornfully. Then, having delivered Miss Mackendrick to her door, she went muttering down the stairs to her basement.

Seven o'clock. Only another hour. The kitchen began to smell pleasantly of food. She filled a large saucepan with water, salted it, and measured the rice into a cup which she placed at the side of the stove. She took knives and forks and napkins – her grandmother's – into the sitting room and put them on the long low table in front of the sofa. The meal suddenly seemed endowed with success. She took the apple tart out of its box and laid it on a baking sheet, ready to go into the oven when the casserole came out.

At seven thirty she lit the gas under the saucepan of

water for the rice. Then she went into the bedroom to repowder her face. She noted with approval that her colour was still high and that her eyes were wide and confident. She felt careless of results now, committed to enjoying the present.

At a quarter to eight she switched off the gas under the pan of water, which was boiling furiously, went into the bathroom and sprayed herself once more with scent. She was extremely hungry but had neglected to buy anything in the way of normal food. There was not so much as a banana in the flat. She made herself a cup of coffee and drank it guiltily, standing at the window, her cheeks flushing deeper with the scalding heat of it. Then there was nothing for it but to refill the pan of water for the rice and start it boiling all over again.

At a quarter past eight she was feeling rather ill. She filled the pan of water yet once more and looked in the oven at her casserole. There was an ominous browning round the edges and she added more wine. She then powdered her face, noting with dismay that her colour had disappeared and that her eyes looked anxious and miserable. Nothing irrevocable has happened, she promised herself, she who was always early. He has been caught in a traffic jam. Or somebody has rung up at the last minute. Or he has had a slow puncture.

At eight thirty she telephoned Anthea to see if Richard had been absent from college that day.

'Oh, Christ,' groaned Anthea. 'Don't ever let this happen again. I can't stand it. Get him to take you out. But don't sit and wait.'

'But if he's ill he can't help it. You can afford not to wait for Brian, you know you can. It's different for me; I've never had a regular boyfriend.'

'Who has?' said Anthea, relapsing from common sense to common despair. 'He'll turn up eventually. Just stick it out. And don't ask him where he's been. Don't bloody well ask him anything. Just don't invite him again, that's all I beg.'

Crashing down the receiver, Ruth walked resolutely to the kitchen, filled the pan of water again, stood over it until it boiled, and with a gesture of supreme recklessness poured in the rice. She then added more water to the casserole, splashing her blouse in the process, and made herself another cup of coffee. She noted in passing that the apple tart was leaking through the pastry crust in the heat. Downstairs she could hear Miss Mackendrick scraping out the cat's litter into the dustbin.

At nine o'clock she felt so ill that she thought she must go to bed. The rice had cooked, stuck, and been thrown away. Wearily she refilled the pan with water and set it to boil. Her dismay was so intense that it was no longer measurable. All she knew was that he did not want to come. He did not want to see her. She did not matter. '*Je suis trop laide, il ne fera pas attention à moi.*' She sat on the sofa in the greyish light, her face as tragic as Helen's when she had played Madame Ranevskaya in *The Cherry Orchard*: her one excursion into serious theatre, and not a success. Ruth thought of her grandmother. She thought of her kind father and her beautiful mother. She had not valued them enough. The following day they would ask how her party had gone. Mrs Cutler would enquire over the outcome of her recipe. Anthea would have to be faced. Accounts must always be rendered, if only to oneself. The effort of holding back her tears blurred and wearied her features. She looked as if she might faint.

At half past nine Miss Howe shuffled out of her basement, the television blaring through her open door, and began her ritual locking up for the night. This involved wrestling with the bolt on the front door, and it would take a great deal of courage to ask her not to do it. Ruth did not bother. She went into the kitchen and poured the water away, switched off the oven, and walked out without clearing up. She turned down her bed and kicked off

54

her shoes. She was beyond feeling anything but relief that the hideous day was over.

At nine thirty five, Richard rang the doorbell.

Miss Howe shot out of her basement, more outraged than frightened. Miss Mackendrick opened her door very slightly, and Ruth could see her small elderly eye through the crack as she ran down the stairs. The blood surged up into her face again; she felt like someone saved from drowning or from a major street accident. The fact that she still had her slippers on, that the dinner was ruined, and that she was so tired that she doubted if she could stay awake much longer did not seem to matter. She would deal with these facts later, after she had appeased Miss Howe.

But she need not have bothered. Richard was already in the hall, stroking Miss Howe's cat, Tiger, and being treated to a confidential report on the state of Tiger's worms. Miss Howe, her thin silver plait of hair undone for the night and hanging down her back, could scarcely afford Ruth a moment's attention.

'You think I should take him to the vet then, do you? I've tried the powders, but he's ailing, you can see it in his eyes.'

Richard draped the cat round his shoulders; Ruth and Miss Howe watched in fascination as he unleashed the full glory of his smile.

'He'll be all right, won't you, old chap?' he said, bringing Tiger down like a scarf until he could rub his cheek on the cat's neck. Tiger was his slave. Miss Howe waited patiently, until he rewarded her with a friendly pat on the shoulder.

Richard being charming again, thought Ruth. Anthea, she knew, would have been less complimentary.

But he was so splendid! Ruth, brought up by parents who did not always hide their exasperation at her inability to grow faster or put on weight, felt inadequate. She did not doubt that the essence of physical attraction lay in a superior degree of beauty, and she knew that she could only wait and wonder that he was there at all. For he had a choice; she had none.

Richard unwound the cat from his neck, bestowed it on Miss Howe, then, raising each foot in a classic gesture, removed his bicycle clips. Tossing them in his hand, and smiling at them, he announced that he was starving. Miss Howe, with Tiger in her arms, seemed reluctant to get back to her television set, and watched them as they both went up the stairs. Then, very slowly, all the doors in the house closed.

If she gave him the melon, Ruth thought, all that was retrievable of the chicken casserole, and most of the apple tart, she could pretend she was not hungry and the day would not be lost. Ramming her feet back into her shoes, she mentally rehearsed an explanation, should he need one. He did not. He ate carefully but not uncritically and did not praise her or thank her. Why should he, she thought. It looked disgusting. The apple tart had finally burst its pastry bounds and she had had to scrape it together and serve it in a pudding bowl. She looked at the fragments longingly; she could have eaten the lot.

'Why don't you relax while I make the coffee?' she said.

He lay full length on the sofa, lit a small cheroot, and closed his eyes.

'Bliss,' he agreed.

I have made him comfortable, Ruth thought, with pride. When she returned with the tray he appeared to be asleep. She placed it carefully on the long low table, then retired to an armchair, uncertain of what to do. Her face, she knew, wore its unredeemed expression again, desirous of pleasing, yet in its very anxiety failing to please. She drank her third, then fourth cup of coffee that evening, replacing the cup quietly in the saucer as if she were in a sickroom.

Richard, with a sudden gesture, raised his head and

56

shoulders, stretched out a hand, drained his cup of coffee, and said, 'No more, thanks,' before sinking back on the sofa, with his arms folded behind his head.

'Dear Ruth,' he said, after a longish pause. 'Tell me what to do.'

'About what?' She felt a little encouraged.

'About so many things. About Harriet, for example.'

'Harriet?'

'Poor girl ran away from home this evening and came to me. That's why I was a bit late, incidentally, I couldn't leave her alone.'

'No, of course not. What's the matter with her?'

'Fed up with her husband. Child getting on her nerves. She just couldn't take any more. I left her in the flat. I suppose I'd better be getting back to her soon.'

'Just a minute,' said Ruth slowly. 'Who's looking after the child?'

'The happy father, I take it. It was his idea to have it. Any fool could see that Harriet wasn't ready for such an experience.'

'Is it very young?'

'Eight months, I think. I'm not too sure.' He laughed. 'Harriet doesn't seem too sure herself.'

'Does Harriet intend to go back?' asked Ruth, who was worried about the sleeping arrangements at Richard's flat.

'I can't let her.' He was suddenly very brisk. 'I think her only hope is to get away from her home surroundings for a bit. She's so confused, poor love. I could send her to these friends of mine in Somerset, but she's not keen.'

Ruth could guess why.

'She's got no money of her own, of course. None of my wretched children have. The thing is, if she went to Somerset, she could make use of the kiln. That's what she really needs, a sense of her own identity. Before her marriage she was a very promising potter.'

57

The small part of Ruth that was still sane wondered why they had to talk about this tiresome person. Surely they had things to say to each other? She thought long-ingly of Helen who always managed to ignore the ex-istence of other women unless she decided to allow them to become her friends. And Anthea! Anthea would not put up with this for one moment. Anthea would be talking about herself. Ruth felt several degrees less worthy than she had at the beginning of the evening. And there was no chance of beginning again; she felt too tired.

'I think Harriet ought to go home,' she said, knowing she was making a mistake. 'She sounds thoroughly spoilt to me.'

Richard unwound his arms from his head, opened his eyes to their fullest extent, and beamed a dark blue gaze in her direction.

'Now I wonder why you said that.' His tone was that of someone catching out a child in a trivial but unbecom-ing offence. 'Just put yourself in her place. Twenty-two years old, saddled with a screaming brat, and a husband who is all set to be something in the city, on tranquilliz-ers, drinking a bit too much, and clearly at the end of her tether. Just to talk to someone about it helped her.'

The wan light of Edith Grove seeped slowly from the room. It was all going wrong. Worse, it had gone wrong. Why should she worry about this Harriet when he was doing it so well all by himself? She had hoped that they might make love, that they might at least make some further plans for meeting again. But instead she was being usurped by Harriet who was not even there. She could not go through this again. But even realizing this, she longed to have the chance to do so.

There was no redeeming the situation and she wanted to be alone.

'What were the other things you were worried about?'

He gave a sigh of genuine heaviness.

58

'So many things, Ruth, so many. Responsibilities and choices all the time. Other people's lives depending on what one says and does.'

She sensed a more immediate, a more intimate danger. Was there an equivalent of 'la jeune Aricie' somewhere in the background? Did she have rivals? Of course, she thought dismally, I must have.

'I still think Harriet ought to go home,' she said, piling the coffee cups on to the tray. 'Even if she didn't want to have a baby she can't refuse to look after it. Anyway, nobody said she had to drink and take tranquillizers. And she could go to evening classes for her pottery.'

Richard, after a minute's silence, relaxed still further on the sofa.

'Sometimes, Ruth,' he murmured, letting his golden-lashed eyelids slowly fall, 'I wonder if you're really a caring person.'

The following day, after a night made sleepless by misery and hunger, she sought him out and forced him to take a cheque for a hundred pounds. This would help Harriet and her ilk to get back to the potter's wheel in Somerset, and would buy food for the unfortunates who had unlimited access to Richard's flat and to his larder. She was well aware that she was paying to remove the stigma of being an uncaring person.

'I don't know when I'll be able to pay you back,' said Richard, who was charmed by her gesture. 'I'll see it gets put into the right hands. By the way, thank you for dinner.'

She would have to move out of Edith Grove and go home, of course. There was no point in keeping the flat on now, and in any case she would be going to France in the autumn. And she would need every penny of the rest of her grandmother's legacy if she wanted to stay in France for a full year. It would be cheaper to pay rent at home.

They were not surprised to see her back. She pretended that the landlord was putting up the rent and that she would not pay it. George helped to move her in the car; the knives and forks were restored to the dining room, the napkins went to the laundry.

'Well,' said Anthea, 'did he turn up?'

'Of course,' said Ruth. 'We had a very interesting evening.' She did not tell Anthea about the cheque. But when she mentioned that she had moved back to Oakwood Court, Anthea refused to speak to her for two whole days.

8

Sally Jacobs's flat in Bayswater was very clean and very warm. Even in September the central heating was on, and with the curtains half pulled to keep the sun out the effect was of entering a seraglio. George, who had taken to driving Mrs Jacobs home from the shop, was pleased with what he saw although he knew it to be in faintly bad taste; this, if anything, increased his pleasure. He particularly delighted in a coffee table covered with a sheet of mirror glass, and when he went into the bathroom to wash his hands he admired the initialled pale green guest towels matching the tooth mugs in plastic opaline. Through the bedroom door he caught a glimpse of a counterpane heavily swagged and pleated in blue-grey satin and a kidney shaped dressing table. The kitchen was immaculate, every surface swept clean of evidence. It looked as if nothing had ever been cooked there, but the battery of mixers, choppers, blenders, and freezers was impressive.

'I make everything myself,' said Mrs Jacobs. 'My ice cream is particularly good. Would you like to try some?'

She gave him a generous helping in a fluted octagonal glass dish which his mother would have relegated to the kitchen, if she had allowed it into the house at all. George basked in the warmth of the flat and the coldness of the ice cream. He particularly liked the way Sally took his plate away the moment he had set it down, how she ran to the kitchen and washed it up. He liked her rather strenuous and obviously expensive silk dresses with their scarves at the neck and their jackets to match; he liked her double string of pearls, worn with the clasp at the side, and her very large diamond ring; he liked the way she talked about her husband.

'Ernest was very good to me,' she said. 'Of course, he was much older than me. More like a father, really. I couldn't say I had a *young* time of it with him. But he looked after me so well. Everything was always taken care of. I never had to make a decision all the time I was married to him.' From her black patent leather bag she extracted a handkerchief generously bordered with lace and wiped her eyes.

George, who had been sitting in his favourite attitude, his legs crossed to show his fine ankles, his face propped up on his hand, the little finger bearing the signet ring with his father's crest slightly raised, felt a long forgotten flicker of desire. Not necessarily for Mrs Jacobs but for the high degree of comfort that seemed to go with her.

He sat down next to her on the sofa, rather heavily; he must watch his weight. He placed a hand over hers and murmured, 'Poor little Sally.' Mrs Jacobs cried harder. George slipped an arm round her and said, 'You know I'll help in any way I can.' And why not? he answered unknown accusers. I have a precious thin time of it at home these days. Sometimes Helen doesn't even bother to get dressed, and as for that woman, she never could cook anyway. And the place is never clean. I've spoiled Helen, that's the truth of it. A woman should look after a man, not the other way round. Papa would never have dreamed of doing anything in the house. I've done enough.

Later Mrs Jacobs made them both a cup of tea, heavily sugared, and served in broad shallow cups. She produced a cut glass jar full of home-made biscuits and draped a tiny embroidered napkin over his knee. George ate hungrily. Down in the car was the half pound of tongue and the tin of artichoke hearts that Mrs Cutler had asked him to bring home for dinner. At least, she had asked for the tongue and something to go with it; George rather fancied himself as a gourmet and they were getting to know him on the ground floor at Fortnum's. He glanced at his watch, registering the time with a start of genuine surprise. They would be well into their drinks at home by now. And that, too, was something they ought to watch.

On the way back to Oakwood Court, driving along with the evening sun on his face, he thought he might buy Sally something to cheer her up. With Ruth at home again, paying rent for her room, Helen did not talk about money as much as she used to. Helen had always been a bit close, in his opinion; he liked a touch of lavishness himself. Helen used to remind him that she earned more than he did. Well, nobody could say that now, since neither of them was earning anything. They were living on the money from the shop, his mother's legacy, and Helen's royalties. Ruth's contribution went straight into the housekeeping.

Sally, he reflected, must be lonely. How could he cheer her up? He had noticed a transistor radio in the kitchen and the largest size of colour television in the sitting room. Perhaps a record player? He could rig it up for her, placing the speakers at what he considered to be ideal intervals. The chairs would have to be moved slightly; no matter. He could spend the odd evening there. No, he admonished himself; they need me at home. He would never get away with it, anyway. But perhaps they could go back to Bayswater in the afternoons? Or he could drive her home a little earlier than usual? Delightful prospects for the winter began to open up in front of him. There was no reason why he should not keep them all happy. And with Ruth at home again, until she went to France – and he really couldn't see why she had to go – there was not much point in his doing the shopping.

He reached home in a fine humour to find Helen and Mrs Cutler having a difference of opinion. It had apparently started shortly after he had left in the late morning and had rumbled on all day. Consequently very little had been done in the flat and last night's washing up was still on the draining board in the kitchen. It was perhaps unfortunate that Helen, wandering in in her nightgown after George's departure, and intending to cut herself a slice of bread and butter, should have knocked over a jar of marmalade which had shattered on the floor. Mrs Cutler, suffering from her usual headache, which lasted until midday, had enjoined Helen, who had wandered back to bed, to clear up the mess. Helen, deprived of her breakfast, and also a little headachy, turned her head very slowly – a gesture for which she had been celebrated in her heyday – and said, 'Darling Maggie, you can't be serious.' She gave a little laugh to indicate incredulity. It was the first bit of acting she had done for some years.

Mrs Cutler, who was no actress, nevertheless had her reserves. Pregnant silences alternating with tuneless whistling, the bathroom door left open, and a refusal to change out of her slippers, eventually modulated into an announcement that there was nothing for lunch and that she was damned if she was going out with all that mess to clear up. Helen then decided that a short course in Christian Science principles might help Maggie to overcome her problems and gave her a small book to read. This had been sent to her by her friend Molly Edwards, an elderly comedy actress now living in retirement in Hove, and relegated to the bedside table where it kept company with several novels by Georgette Heyer.

'I found it *immensely* helpful,' said Helen, knocking the dust from it and presenting it to Mrs Cutler. 'And could we have a cup of tea?'

'No time, if I'm going to read this,' replied Mrs Cutler with great satisfaction. She could go without food indefinitely. She not only read it, she read it aloud, frequently popping in to ask Helen's advice on a passage with which she disagreed. They were both enjoying themselves in a dangerous kind of way and it seemed only natural that they should have a heated discussion of some of the finer points over a large whisky. After all, they could not eat until George came home with the food. As they had had nothing all day the drinks went to their heads, and their voices were raised when George put his key in the door. Mamma always knew when I was coming home, he thought.

George exerted himself to calm the two women down but could barely intervene in their debate, which had now reached major proportions. Leaving them to it, he retired to the kitchen and made the tongue up into sandwiches, arranging them carefully on a plate. He went to the dining room and fetched three of his mother's napkins, stiff with starch; these he added to the tray which he took into the bedroom. He placed the tray on the bed, between Helen and Mrs Cutler, who both reached out a hand automatically and went on talking.

'I have lost more than you have ever had,' said Helen imperiously, 'yet I remain buoyant, optimistic.'

Mrs Cutler revealed a fine head for argument.

'If it's all in the mind, who said you ever had it?' she countered.

'My success is as real as your bunions,' retorted Helen furiously. 'And we hear enough about those.'

The technical victory was Mrs Cutler's.

'It says here that neither exists,' she said, laying down her tongue sandwich to find the source of her conclusion in Mrs Eddy's text.

Helen laid the back of her wrist to her forehead – a gesture for which she had also been famous – and said 'I cannot bear it,' in so genuinely broken a voice that Mrs Cutler shot her a glance and retired to the kitchen to do last night's washing up. George, reluctantly replacing his sandwich, put his arm round Helen to comfort her.

'Come on, darling heart, it's not like you to give way like this.'

Helen, who was picking the meat out of his bread and eating it, rallied.

'It's just that I get so tired listening to her stories about her beastly marriage and her beastly feet.'

At this point Mrs Cutler came in with another tray, bearing the *amende honorable*: three plates of sliced tinned peaches. She had intended to offer them coffee, but thought better of it.

'I'll have an early night if it's all the same to you,' she said, tight-lipped.

'Yes, do, darling,' urged Helen. 'You'll feel better in the morning.'

She was feeling much better herself, and allowed herself an extra sleeping pill as a treat. She was quite ready to settle down after so stimulating a day.

When Ruth returned from her usual long walk later that evening, she discovered George in the kitchen eating artichoke hearts out of the tin. He looked furtive but not unhappy. She kissed him goodnight and went silently to her room. George, smiling, allowed himself one of his late father's cigars.

9

In the evenings Ruth walked. She was too lonely to sit in her room reading, too restless to work. She went down to Edith Grove and started walking from there, down to the river, along the embankment to Chelsea Old Church, all the way to Victoria and back to Sloane Square and along the King's Road and into the Fulham Road until it got too late and she caught the 31 bus home. The weather was superb: a golden autumn such as she could not remember. The streets were tranquil; knots of young people dedicated to love and peace strolled along or drank their beer on the pavements outside the pubs. In the cooling dusk she was not disturbed.

She had never found the long vacation so difficult before. Usually she worked in the even more silent library, well pleased with her steady progress, her growing involvement with her characters. But now things were different. Work was a refuge and she found herself unable to seek that particular sort of asylum. Work, she thought, is a paradox: it is the sort of thing people do out of sheer inability to do anything else. Work is the chosen avocation of those who have no other calls on their time.

She did not really mind being at home. It was anonymous, familiar; she had no further need for independence. Her recent encounter with reality had shocked her and made her feel childish. Only her books and her notes allowed her some measure of dignity, but there was no one waiting to read her essays or to question her on the psychology of *Le Misanthrope*; alone with her work, she felt a regretful distaste for so much unacknowledged effort. That this was but a shadow of a much stronger regret she was not yet fully aware. She only knew that she found it hard to fill the time. Anthea and Brian had gone off to Greece. Richard was with his friends in Somerset: no doubt the wretched Harriet was being listened to still further. Even Mrs Cutler had spent the previous weekend with her sister-in-law, whom she loathed, in Totteridge ('Beautiful place she's got there. Just like the country.'). In her absence Ruth had done the cooking but had not enjoyed it. 'Fabulous, darling,' said Helen, her mouth full of chicken casserole, but she went back to bed as soon as the meal was finished, leaving Ruth and her father at the kitchen table with very little to say to each other.

A London summer. She had had many. Holidays were rare in the Weiss household. When she was a child her grandmother had taken her to those mild watering places that she herself had known in earlier days: the Isle of Wight to recover from measles and chicken pox, then Baden Baden, Vevey, Scheveningen. They had sat obediently in hotel gardens and lounges, planning their walks, their rests, looking forward only to the hours between tea and dinner. Sometimes a band would play. Once they took the train from Vevey to Montreux, where her grandmother had spent her honeymoon; once they took a lake steamer in the other direction. Rousseau and Stendhal had left their mark here, but Ruth was too young and they did not yet matter. At Scheveningen they sat huddled in the chill wind in the Kurhaus gardens. Ruth had only once braved the sea, while her grandmother stood guard on the endless and almost untenanted beach.

While they sipped their tea in Baden Baden – her grandmother with an old-fashioned sunshade and Ruth's pullover on her knee – George and Helen went on tour or stayed with friends in Menton. They were good guests, Helen so vivacious, George so good-natured. But all that had come to an end. Baden Baden and Vevey were still there, Ruth did not doubt; even the improbable Scheveningen was still reachable. But Oakwood Court, now permanently occupied, as if they were under house arrest, had assumed a centrality that had never existed before. The elder Mrs Weiss had imposed calm and order. Now there was a restlessness of continuous yet undignified occupation. They could not get away.

Ruth sensed danger here, if only because she herself had so little to report after her vacations. For how could she talk about wandering the evening streets between Kensington and Victoria? Occasionally she went to Paris, not too often because her parents always reacted with dismay if she appeared to be leaving them. But she knew that Paris was not the answer, for she pursued her same dreamy paths there, or sat in the Luxembourg Gardens as if her grandmother were still beside her with the sunshade and the spare pullover. And getting home was no relief either, for she had so little to say for herself. 'Well,' Anthea would demand, 'did anything happen?' Nothing happened.

It was with this knowledge that nothing was happening that Ruth returned to Oakwood Court one evening in mid-September and informed her parents in a tone of nannyish cheerfulness that they should go away for a holiday. That it would do them good. That they spent too much time in the flat. That they did not see enough people. That she would be off herself in October and that she would like to see them looking fit and refreshed before she left. George was deeply annoyed. Helen was amazed. Mrs Cutler was all in favour.

George was annoyed because he found himself unwilling to spend any money, having already spent a good deal in the electrical department at Peter Jones. The record player, which he had not yet presented to Mrs

Jacobs, had cost more than he expected but the euphoria of spending his own money had got out of hand, and he had gone on to treat himself to a sun lamp and a small portable grill in which, the assistant told him, he could make toasted sandwiches. He planned to keep these two items at Sally's flat; he could see himself fit and bronzed from the sun lamp and lean and trim from the steaks with which he would supply the grill. He would have to ring Peter Jones to postpone the date on which he intended to have the things sent to Bayswater. He had warned Sally to expect a couple of bulky packages and had mistaken the look of alarm that flashed across her face for one of pleasure and awe. He did not feel he could go on eating her ice cream and biscuits without making some sort of return. And he did so love to see her face, with her large, anxious, and rather protuberant eyes, scanning the street from between snowy flounces of Terylene at the window, for his departing wave. Why should he need a holiday? He was already having one.

Helen was more receptive to the idea, though not in any practical sense. The mere mention of the word holiday sent her on a bout of reminiscences, mainly of late nights, fast cars, dancing in the waves with a glass of gin in her hand, and someone to iron her evening dress.

'Well, we can't go to Menton,' said George. 'We can't afford it.'

'I believe Freddy sold his place to a retired juke box manufacturer,' replied Helen. 'Hideous, isn't it, the way everything gets worse?'

Mrs Cutler was in favour of the coast, any coast. Wales, she said generously, Scotland. It did not have to be abroad. Ruth thought this not a bad idea. She felt that her parents needed to recover some vigour and muscularity and the idea of healthful walks in a sea breeze was uppermost in her mind. She perceived in them some fundamental loss of tone that made her uneasy. She wanted to get them repaired, as it were, before she left

70

them behind.

'I don't mind where we go, as long as it's not those bloody fjords,' said Helen, closing her eyes.

'There is no question of fjords,' said George, who had always wanted to see them, and who had mentioned them at intervals throughout his married life. 'There is no question of Freddy's place, whether it's there or not. We really have to pull in our horns. There is no money coming in, remember.'

Helen opened her eyes and looked serious, as she always did at the mention of money.

'In that case,' she mused, 'we'd better go down to Molly at Hove. She's always dying to see us.'

This was a slight exaggeration. Molly Edwards, carmined lips stretched resolutely in a smile, flabby upper arms and thighs fearlessly revealed by a flowered bathing suit, was the Christian Science practitioner who had tried to convert Helen, with no success. Molly herself found that she needed to spend a good deal of time on her own if only to keep her philosophy of life a going concern. From her ground floor flat at the remoter end of the Hove seafront she would emerge every morning, rain or shine, in her bathing dress, covered with a towelling wrap; she would be carrying an oilcloth bag which contained her library book, her copy of the *Christian Science Monitor*, and her lunch, a banana sandwich and an apple. She would repair to her beach chalet, a small hut fitted with a garden chair and an electric kettle, and there she would sit all the morning, reading and sipping tea, until midday when she plunged into the sea and swam vigorously for half an hour. People thought she was wonderful for her age, although she did not look it as she picked her wet chilled way back over the shingle after her bathe. But a quick rub of her short grey hair with a towel, another cup of tea, and she was herself again, ignoring the increasing fibrositis that made swimming so deeply unpleasant. And perhaps she was right. Perhaps she would have felt worse if she sat around all day thinking about it. In any event she took another bathe just after four in the afternoon, then locked up the hut and went home. She ate mostly health foods, for which she shopped in bulk every Saturday. She had no desire to have her routine interrupted, fond though she was of Helen, to whom she had recently sent a photograph of herself, smiling gallantly, arms akimbo, with the sea as a background.

'God, doesn't she look ghastly?' was Helen's reaction.

So somehow it was decided that Helen and George should spend ten days with Molly at Hove. Mrs Cutler promised to have the bedroom done out while they were away, and took Helen to the hairdresser so as to make a good and enviable impression on her old friend, whom she had not seen for some years. Ruth found herself in charge of the packing, and was filled with amazed pity as she went through the jumble of dingy luxurious clothes in tallboys and wardrobes. There was no time to have them cleaned but she ironed them all assiduously. George, immaculate, was packed in less than an hour.

Nevertheless, there was a considerable amount of luggage. And as Helen refused to travel long distances by car, claiming that they made her feel sick, Ruth, with some misgivings, purchased two first class return tickets and arranged for a taxi from a car-hire firm to take them to Victoria. The day of their departure dawned warm and misty; it was going to be very hot. Helen, stumbling around in unaccustomed shoes and not too steady on her feet these days, left half-smoked cigarettes burning in saucers as she searched ineffectually for a chiffon scarf or the novel she was nearly through or for the half bottle of brandy she was never without on her travels. George, scented with aftershave, crisp white handkerchief stuck up his sleeve, *The Times* in his airline shoulder bag, whistled to himself on the pavement, trying to believe that ten days would go in a flash. Helen, her face chalky in the now radiant morning light, climbed unsteadily into the taxi; George's signet ring flashed in the sunlight as he turned to wave goodbye to Ruth and Mrs Cutler in the porch. Ruth felt a lurch of fear. Would they manage at Victoria? Her mother was so unused to crowds. Mrs Cutler sensed her anxiety. 'Do them good,' she said firmly. 'They're as sheltered as a couple of kids. Do them good to get buffeted about a bit.' She seemed to like the idea. To George and Helen, now two faces at the window of the taxi, she raised her thumb in an all-purpose gesture. 'Never say die,' she yelled cheerfully, and went indoors to change back into her slippers.

10

To her surprise, Ruth found that she got on rather well with Mrs Cutler. They had a sort of holiday of their own. After turning out the bedroom and retrieving from under the bed a year's accumulation of spilt and crushed pills, old tissues, and the crosswords torn out of the Sunday papers, they felt a glow of achievement. The room was thoroughly aired and then just as thoroughly closed. By tacit consent they agreed that too much time was spent in there. 'There's that nice drawing room,' said Mrs Cutler. 'I'm the only one that ever sees it.' She cleaned that out too, taking down the curtains and wheeling them to the coin-operated machine at the local launderette. Ruth returned to the dining room, removed the stained damask cloth that still covered half the table from last Sunday's lunch, opened the windows and let out the stale air. There had never been such an autumn.

'Aren't they lucky?' said Mrs Cutler. 'I'll bet they're laughing at us here in London.'

'Mother looked awfully frail, I thought.' Ruth hesitated. The sight of her mother's white face had stayed in her mind.

'A bit too much of this,' replied Mrs Cutler, lifting her elbow. 'That and lounging about all day. She's out of touch. Sea air will do her a power of good. You won't know her when she comes back.'

Ruth wished to believe it. She would indeed have welcomed back parents whom she did not know. The bedroom with its detritus had left a disagreeable impression on her; it was as if they had cleared up after a death. Ruth was glad of Mrs Cutler, with her hoarse smoker's cough, her rakish thinness, her obvious durability. She offered to do the shopping while Mrs Cutler put her feet up. She was determined to become a good cook. Mrs Cutler, unexpectedly, showed her how to make a perfect egg custard. Ruth, in her turn, helped Mrs Cutler to apply her home hair dye, out of a bottle with a twenty-year-old brunette smiling alluringly from the label. 'Chestnut lights,' she read out. 'Shampoo once, rinse, then shampoo in the solution and wait for half an hour.' Mrs Cutler looked apprehensive. Ruth sat with her, putting out a restraining hand as Mrs Cutler kept glancing at her watch. Under the plastic shower cap orange rivulets began to trickle down her forehead. The result, when washed out, was not much different from Mrs Cutler's ordinary hair, but Ruth persuaded her to abandon her ochreous powder and crimson lipstick for something more becoming, and was quite pleased with her appearance. She looked more acceptable, less like a saloon bar habituée. Her grandmother would have nodded approval.

Some mornings Mrs Cutler volunteered to do the shopping, but Ruth liked to get out. An urge to stay all day in the divine air of late September was like a physical quickening of her blood. Almost, she was happy. Or perhaps she recognized that this was how happiness felt. All one needed was a pretext. If there were no pretext, one needed an analogue. But Ruth, walking endlessly, was content to experience the unlooked for exhilaration, to hope, to beg, that one day, some day, she might find a reason for feeling as she did, buoyant, serene, anaesthetized against everyday hurts. She imagined, wrongly, that being in love was like this. With love comes seriousness, loss of autonomy, responsibility without power. Love, Ruth thought wistfully, must surely be this state of

75

sublime ease. She even thought that before she left for France she might get in touch with Richard. But perhaps he would think she wanted the money back? Regretfully, she abandoned the idea and the bright day darkened a little. Without love, there can be no reason for hope.

She began to think seriously about going to France. A room had been secured for her in the La Muette flat of Humphrey and Rhoda Wilcox whom George counted among his most faithful customers. Humphrey wrote popular lives of French favourites: *La Vie passionnée de Madame de Sévigné* and *Robespierre, cet inconnu* still sold pretty successfully in bookshops near the Palais Royal. Rhoda was fashion correspondent for various Scottish papers. Apart from these racy activities, they were an elderly and rather severe couple. Ruth remembered them vaguely from a visit they had paid to Oakwood Court when she was much younger. She did not much like the idea of living with them – or indeed with anyone – but George had been insistent.

'You will be quite independent,' he assured Ruth. 'You will be living in the maid's room which I understand is on the top floor. And I can always get in touch with you: Rhoda and Humphrey are on the telephone.'

'Sounds like a dead loss to me,' said Mrs Cutler, who would be confirmed in her opinion if she ever met them. Rhoda, thin and beautiful like Helen, but much older, was dedicated to the preservation of Humphrey, who was even older and who was currently engaged on a life of the Duchesse de Berry. So much Ruth had gleaned from George's description. Mrs Cutler quite rightly inferred that they would not welcome interruptions, that telephone calls would be rationed and morals supervised. Ruth did not much care. As long as the weather lasted she could be out all day and if anything happened (to use Anthea's phrase) she would look for another flat. The main thing was that she had an address: 154 rue des Marronniers, and any letters that arrived for her could be sent on there. She decided to leave on October 4th.

For a week the glorious weather continued in all its power and strength: milky white mornings, pale sun at ten o'clock, fire at midday. Even Mrs Cutler succumbed to its allure and consented to take tea with Ruth in Holland Park. They fed the birds and watched the babies, two women on their own, even in each other's company, but peaceable and not noticeably discontented.

'I wonder how they're getting on,' said Ruth. They had had no word, apart from a telephone call from Molly Edwards to tell them that George and Helen had arrived safely. Molly had sounded so tremendously cheerful and optimistic that Mrs Cutler, who had tried the ways of Christian Science and found them wanting, suspected that something had already gone terribly wrong. But she said nothing, not wishing to spoil Ruth's holiday. And her own, of course.

'Forgotten all about us by now, I shouldn't wonder,' said Mrs Cutler.

She was nearly right. The taxi had unloaded George and Helen into a maelstrom of returning holiday makers, a world they did not known existed: elderly men with veins standing out on their foreheads trying to cope with five suitcases, elderly women with swollen feet and glistening white cardigans bought especially for the holiday, enduring the fright of a lifetime in order to enjoy the pleasure they had promised themselves all the winter, too many children, shrill with tiredness, their long hair sticking to their damp faces, their mouths smeared and stained with sweets, none of them aspiring even to the relative comfort of a taxi, but queuing patiently for buses, shifting their burdens from hand to hand, trying to quieten the children, longing for that cup of tea at home, safe at last for another year.

'Good God,' said Helen, emerging from the taxi at Victoria. 'Where on earth do they all come from? I have never seen such people in my life.'

George, assembling the luggage, rather agreed with her but wished she would not stare. The back of Helen's wrist drifted up to her forehead. One or two people, vaguely remembering her face from the cinema, wondered who she was. Helen was torn between the desire to make an entrance, to plunge into the throng as if it were assembled outside the stage door, and the desire to be taken care of. Her predicament was solved when she caught sight of the open doors of an ambulance, which had evidently just delivered someone on to a train. The two ambulance men, wiping their mouths, returning from a tea break, prepared to pack up and drive off. Helen tottered convincingly. 'George,' she said, in the voice that had once carried to the back of the stalls. 'I think I'm going to faint.'

George was ashamed of her, as he was so often these days, but as Helen was conveyed in a wheelchair to the Brighton platform – and not engaging even a ripple of attention, she was annoyed to see – he struggled after her with the luggage, thankful at least that she was sitting down. She would be all right now, he knew; she would have a triumph to recount. That usually did the trick.

The journey down was relatively easy, though George did not get his crossword done. Helen was being very charming to a thin woman sitting in the corner of the carriage, although the thin woman was nervous and clearly wanted to read her book.

'Anything interesting?' asked Helen, who intended to talk.

'Henry James,' replied the thin woman repressively.

'You'll never believe this,' said Helen, 'but I once played the niece, Miss Whatsit, in *The Aspern Papers*. We toured it. Brighton, in fact. Do you remember, darling heart? George?' Newspaper and book were laid aside. Helen lit a cigarette, ignoring the fact that they were in a non-smoking compartment, and entertained them with anecdotes. Brighton was reached in comparative amity.

It was at Brighton station that the trouble started. Molly Edwards, cheerful and spartan with her beach hut and health foods, did not possess a car. They joined another queue for a taxi, and when crushed into it, were informed by Molly that she had had to put them up in the dining room, as her lodger, now on holiday, had not removed his belongings from the spare bedroom. Why should he? He had paid the rent. What she did not say was that the lodger occupied the only bedroom, and that she herself slept on a divan in the drawing room: they all shared the kitchen. Took it in turns, said Molly firmly. She had no intention of cooking meat but of course would not object if they wanted to cook it themselves.

'Good Christ,' exploded Helen. 'What do you want a dining room for, Molly? You could eat a nut cutlet or whatever it is you eat off a tray.'

'I can't get rid of the furniture,' said Molly. And indeed she couldn't. There was a highly varnished gate-legged table dating from the nineteen-thirties, a china cabinet filled with wedding presents of the same epoch, and six chairs in heavy leather embossed with gilt studs. Nobody would either buy them or take them away. Molly had made an effort. She had shut up the table and ranged the chairs against one wall. In the remaining floor space stood two very narrow divan beds, a small table, and a lamp with a dull parchment shade and a long trailing flex. Helen took one look and raised the back of her hand to her forehead. This time the gesture was entirely genuine.

George thought longingly of Mrs Jacobs's flat, of the entryphone and the door chimes and the electric blanket and the frilled nylon pillowslips he had seen airing in the bathroom. He thought of the record player and the sun lamp and the towelling bathrobe he intended to hang on the back of the bedroom door. You never knew. Molly, putting on the kettle, thought with equal longing of her cool expanse of beach and her chalet and the *Christian*

Science Monitor and its injunctions. She had tried. She had baked a sodden fruit loaf for them. After that they were on their own. The smell of Helen's cigarette and the sound of her lamentations drifted ominously into Molly's consciousness. Well, it was only for ten days. It was a change, wasn't it?

In the bedroom or dining room – it looked like neither – Helen was taking a pull at her bottle of brandy. She had removed some dried grasses from a large green vase and was using it as an ashtray. Her shoes were off and she was lying on her divan with a distant look in her eye.

'Tomorrow,' she said to George, 'we go home.'

At this point Molly entered with the tea and a scrapbook. Ignoring the signs of Helen's occupancy, she said, 'You'll never guess, darling. I found some photographs of you the other day. Look how beautiful you were.' Helen sat up. 'Still are, of course,' said Molly. She was quite sincere.

Helen pondered.

'I was just saying to George, we shall have to leave before the weekend. Our daughter is going to France soon and we want to spend as much time as possible with her.'

'That tiny little thing? Of course you do,' said kind Molly. 'A bit of sea air and you'll look quite different when you get home. You could do with a swim or two, my girl. Why not come down to the beach with me to-morrow? George can bring a couple of deckchairs over from the bandstand.'

Helen bowed to the inevitable. Reaching out for the scrapbook she said, 'Is there a photograph of me in *Most Loving Mere Folly*? They say I looked my best then.'

Leaving the two women sitting side by side and apparently in harmony for the moment, George went out to get the supper.

Helen made one effort to join in the spirit of what she

contemptuously called 'your seaside home' by buying herself a curious peaked denim cap at the local beach shop and by wearing it both indoors and out through the seemingly endless days that followed. Ushered down to the chalet by Molly, she had stared at her friend in amazement.

'You mean to tell me you sit here all the time? But Molly, you must be mad. You could still get work. What about those talking books for the blind? They're always on at me to record some, but I can't seem to get round to it.'

Molly smiled sadly.

'I'm not as young as I was. I'm older than you, remember, Helen. I've got just enough to keep me until I pop off, and then that's it. Remember what we used to say? No regrets.'

'No regrets,' echoed Helen. She was more shaken than she would admit. Her friend was a living embodiment of all that awaited her. Helen knew that was ageing badly, that she had lost too much weight, that her teeth ached, that her circulation was bad. Sometimes she kept her make-up on all night in order not to give herself a shock the following morning. It was only by resting most of the day, by eating soft foods that did not demand too much effort, by never risking the challenges of the street, of the bus, that she kept as well as she did. It suited her looks to never quite get dressed, to trail, to chatter, to heighten the colour of her eye sockets and her cheeks, and above all to sleep. She had brought her pills with her to Hove, of course. But she felt brittle, exposed, chilled by the invigorating wind off the sea. Her wedding ring slipped about on her finger. She could think of nothing to do. She remembered that she was older than George. She was almost frightened. And her face wore that lost and petulant air that Ruth remembered from her childhood and which seemed to turn the mother into the child and the child into the mother.

George, too, was far from happy. He left the two women together and walked into Brighton: at least he could keep himself in shape. On the walk back he did the shopping. He longed, with a fierceness that surprised him, to sit down at a decent table and have someone serve his food. He longed to eat a meal without knowing in advance what it was. He longed, if not for Sally, then for life in Sally's flat. Sometimes he caught himself longing for his mother. Ruth would have recognized his expression too: rueful, withdrawn, the lips pursed. A stranger, suddenly.

The sun came out and they made a slight effort. George hired a car and they drove along the coast. They had lunch in restaurants and tea in hotels. Then George realized how much money they were spending and announced that they should take more advantage of the open air. They had come for the sea bathing, after all.

'You hate it,' said Helen. 'You always have.'

'I'm quite happy,' replied George, 'sitting here in the chalet.' While he sat there he let his anger mount and felt it was doing him a power of good. Anger would liberate him from servility, would make him lose his scruples. Anger, he almost believed, would enable him to have his own way.

Following in Molly's crunching wake over the beach, Helen tried not to look at the blade-like thinness of her own legs. Her narrow feet, now unused to walking, turned at the ankle and she wondered how she would ever get back. As she hobbled thankfully over the rim of sand into the sea the shock of the water nearly took her breath away. The waves were boisterous and her knees gave way. Water slopped over her mouth; her hair, so carefully set for the holiday, straggled in wet strands on her neck. Without her looks she felt her personality deteriorate. Molly, splashing cheerfully and trying to ignore the pain in her shoulder, shouted, 'You'll feel the benefit later.'

As he helped to dry her, rubbing her bluish white feet while Molly shook herself like a dog and plugged in the kettle, George knew that he no longer loved his wife. He felt – and this he had always felt, although he did not know the reason – extremely sorry for her. As a natural corollary, he felt extremely sorry for himself. He was still vigorous; he did not think of himself as an ageing man. His looks had not changed noticeably since his mother died. He still eyed himself appreciatively in the glass every morning. He had, he felt, a future. With Mrs Jacobs. He would tell Helen that he was going to buy a share in the bookshop and spend his time there. The others would have to make their own arrangements. Ruth, if necessary, could stay at home. All this flashed through his mind with a rapidity that amazed him. When the moment of revelation passed – really, this holiday was doing them no good at all – he knew that he could not carry out all his plans, put all his projects into effect. But some . . . Why not some?

Helen, with frozen hands, jammed on her peaked cap. They were all, for various reasons, subdued. Then Molly, against every principle she held dear, reached into her canvas hold-all and produced a bottle of gin.

Helen turned to her, with her beautiful smile restored. 'Molly, my darling, you are an angel. Always were. Never jealous or ratty. Not even when I had that little affair with Eric.'

Molly had not known about this. She had trusted her late husband implicitly. But she was a sensible woman; she saw in Helen's face the end of many love affairs. We shall none of us ever make love again, she thought, and did not much care. Life had not been too harsh. The sea would still be there at the end. She was nearly ready.

But Helen, she saw, would be taken unawares.

11

Ruth, trying to put her notes into some kind of order, realized that the days were getting shorter. She could no longer walk in the evenings. Leaves were being raked and burnt in back gardens; from midday to three in the afternoon the sun still blazed and clothes felt too heavy. Then the brightness went out of the air; the light, with infinite slowness, receded into a greyish mist; the smoke rose from the gardens and drifted round the trees. As dusk came down, late roses startled with the intensity of their colour.

Ruth, in her bedroom, struggled with *Modeste Mignon*, in which all the vices turn out to be virtues. Mrs Cutler, at the kitchen table, studied her horoscope in the evening paper. The flat was clean, the store cupboard provisioned. In Ruth's wardrobe hung a new blue dress in which she planned to take Paris by storm, for had not Balzac laid that obligation upon her? Her ticket was booked, Humphrey and Rhoda Wilcox alerted. She was in two minds about going. Oakwood Court was now so peaceful that she felt she might work here quite as well as in the Wilcoxes' maid's room. The quality of life had improved quite a bit. Mrs Cutler was now watching cookery programmes on afternoon television, but as she never wrote down the recipes there was little chance of her ever reproducing them. She regarded them as pure entertainment, in the same way as she sat through programmes about woodland predators or crime on the streets of New York.

'The kitchens they must have,' she marvelled. 'And fancy eating all those courses at one meal.'

They had both benefited greatly from the holiday in Hove.

It was therefore with something like dismay that they became aware that the surge of the lift and the noise of its doors slamming meant that George and Helen were home.

Their eyes met over the kitchen table. Neither moved. Cautiously, Mrs Cutler diminished the volume of her transistor radio. In the hall voices were raised, lights switched on, and a stumbling struggle, in which cases were dropped or even dragged, dominated the whine of bullets from the detective play to which they were listening.

'Never again,' they could hear Helen groaning, 'never again.'

Reaching out a hand, Mrs Cutler turned off the radio and they both, resignedly, got to their feet.

'It was ghastly,' said Helen the following morning from her bed, although she seemed quite cheerful. 'Sitting in that dog kennel all day with the monsoon blowing and Molly's cooking sticking permanently in one's teeth. Why are vegetarians so unreasonable?'

George and Ruth and Mrs Cutler had reassembled in the bedroom, which had resumed its air of disorder and permanence. Suitcases had been opened but not unpacked. An open bottle of nail varnish, its brush already stiff, added a strong smell to the already stale air. Helen wore her denim cap, her nightdress, and a cardigan, and was lighting one cigarette from the stub of another. George lined up the pair of shoes from which Helen had thankfully removed her feet the previous evening. After a moment's hesitation he threw them under the bed. Ruth observed him as he picked minute pieces of fluff

85

from the sleeve of his jacket. He seemed quieter than usual.

Ruth thought that something in her parents had changed but could not identify the change. Physically, they were both very much present. They seemed to be occupying more space than usual. Perhaps she had got used to the relative silence of Mrs Cutler. Perhaps being in the open air had made them seem so voluble, so oppressive.

'Now that you're home,' said Ruth, 'you mustn't slip into bad habits again. You're much too lazy, Mother. You should get out more.'

Helen turned her head very slowly.

'Get out?' she questioned. 'I don't even feel like getting up.'

That was it; that was the change. Helen meant it. They all knew that she meant it. Something would have to be done. But Ruth remembered her mother's face as she had seen it the previous evening, frightened and old under the unbecoming slant of the peaked cap. George had seen it too. Mrs Cutler had seen it and was determined to do something about it.

Mrs Cutler had liked being mistress of the flat: she didn't count Ruth. She remembered a time when she had been mistress of her own small house in Battersea, when Douglas would take her to the pub on a Friday evening, when she had a captive audience of her own. The only stratagem she knew took shape in her mind. She was not keen on it but it would have to do.

'I've been thinking,' she said, unconsciously fingering her left hand. 'I might like to get married again. Can't give up without trying, can you?'

George was stunned. Helen, on the contrary, seemed very sympathetic. She foresaw entertainment for the weeks ahead. And she need not even get up for it.

'There are marriage bureaux, of course,' said Helen. 'I believed there's one next to Barker's. Why don't you sign on or fill in the form or whatever you have to do, and then you can ask them back here, whoever they are. If anyone turns up,' she added kindly. 'As you know, I'm a pretty good judge of character. And men are such liars; they certainly won't tell you the truth. But they won't get much past me.' She seemed cheered by the prospect. 'With my experience,' she said.

Mrs Cutler, who had already decided to take her project seriously but to meet any aspirants at the Mexicana coffee bar next door to the launderette, agreed to let Helen help her with the application.

'Say you're of independent means,' advised Helen, now filled with enthusiasm. 'That always gets them. And, after all, you are, aren't you?'

Ruth slipped out of the room as her father was leaving.

'Is she all right?' she asked. 'She looks different, somehow. Thinner, more highly coloured.'

'Of course she's all right,' replied George. They were whispering. He was annoyed. Nobody worried how *he* was. He was becoming restive.

'I don't like the idea of your going away, Ruth. Don't like it at all. Especially if Maggie's going to leave.'

Ruth looked at him in astonishment.

'But who on earth would want to marry Mrs Cutler?' she asked. 'She doesn't mean it. This is the only home she's ever likely to have.'

George shook his head.

'Think about it, Ruth. You have a duty to her, you know.' Then he left, in a hurry to get to Peter Jones, to oversee his purchases and perhaps buy himself a towelling bathrobe.

This was the first Ruth had heard of her duty, which she had always imagined was confined to the characters of Balzac. She had a duty to them, certainly, and the British Council, no less, had recognized it. Her father could not really imagine that she would be of any use here?

87

In the days that followed, it became quite clear that he did.

On the first Tuesday in October, in an atmosphere of suppressed disappointment and anxiety, Ruth waited for the taxi to take her to Victoria Station. Her mother was in bed ('You don't mind, do you, darling heart? My precious girl? I am just a *little* bit tired'). Her father, who was gravely displeased with her, had gone to Mount Street to prove it. Ruth was suddenly bereft. As her taxi drew up and she prepared to say goodbye to Oakwood Court, she glanced up at the window of the dining room. There she saw Mrs Cutler, watchful and pinched once again, her chestnut lights faded, her lipstick incarnadine. Behind her stretched a day already full of instant coffee.

Mrs Cutler raised her thumb. Ruth could not make out the words she was mouthing. Her throat ached, her eyes burned with loneliness. She waved. Mrs Cutler threw open the window.

'Keep in touch,' she shouted, thinly, so as not to attract the attention of the neighbours. Ruth could barely hear her. 'Make the most of it,' yelled Mrs Cutler, getting into the spirit of the thing. 'Go on, Ruth don't hang about.' She raised her thumb again. 'Never say die!' And she slammed down the window.

12

Ruth woke up, sat up, and eased herself into another day
in the rue des Marronniers. She reached for her notebook
and wrote down her dream, having read in a magazine
that this was therapeutic. The dream, as usual, had been
disagreeable. She had been waiting in a freezing cold
bed-sitting room, painted white, for her examination
results. She knew, with a deep and ancient inner conviction, that all the other rooms in the house were heated,
and all the other occupants were in receipt of good news.
Before she could be moved to begin her usual mild
protest against this state of affairs, she was translated to
Brussels, where an enormous hunger overcame her. She
was so busy bolting down coffee and rolls that she could
not spare the time to entertain her companion, a person
of indeterminate sex with grey hair. She awoke, bewildered, in the knowledge that she had been left alone at the
café table while her companion set off with purposeful
gestures to cross a small wood or garden thickly carpeted
with fallen leaves. This dream had been in colour. Rather
like a film.

In contrast to her dream, the sepia light that strained to
get through the barred window of her room on the sixth
floor in the rue des Marronniers reduced her life to
monochrome. She still could not believe that anyone had
consigned her to this place when she had committed no
crime. Although Rhoda and Humphrey Wilcox had been
severe and owlish enough to inspire a certain discomfort,

she had liked their bright chintzy flat and had looked forward to leading a quiet life there. Rhoda had given her a cup of tea and a very small biscuit, had steered her towards the eighty-year-old Humphrey who was sitting, tortoise-like, in his armchair, and had left her to do something in the kitchen. Ruth had been aware that this was the equivalent of one of those country house weekends at which you are assessed for your suitability to occupy a minor but significant post in the Civil Service. Ignoring Humphrey's hand, which strayed towards her knee and rested there, ignoring his insistence on speaking French – he wrote his biographies under the pseudonym of Maurice de Grandville – she listened for twenty minutes to his disquisition on the life of the Duchesse de Berry, and would have listened longer had they both not become aware of Rhoda, returned from the kitchen, and standing with folded arms by the door. Humphrey removed his hand, which was pale and humid, like that of a poulterer.

'Humphrey has quite taken to you,' said Rhoda. 'I think it will be all right to let you have the room, although Humphrey sometimes meditates up there. You do know about maids' rooms, don't you?'

Ruth shook her head. 'I only know they're usually on the top floor.'

'At one time all the servants in the building had the top floor to themselves. No servants now, of course, but there is a staircase outside the kitchen door which they all used when they started work in the mornings. So much more civilized than having them living in.'

She led Ruth, with her suitcase and her typewriter, out through the kitchen door, up the staircase, and along an endless prison corridor which appeared to have small cells opening off it at regular intervals. She fitted a large iron key into an obdurate door, forced it open, and went over to push back the shutters of the window. This made no appreciable difference to the quality of light in the room, which was furnished with a double bed, a small papier mâché table, and a sink with a jaunty little screen round it. One cold tap.

'You're extremely lucky to find the room empty,' said Rhoda, peering at Ruth narrowly as if she were indeed a servant, were up to no good, and might possibly be pregnant. She was a queenly and reproving woman who made Ruth feel apologetic. Although, she said to herself, the boot is really on the other foot; I'm paying good money for this.

'My nephew usually has the room when he comes over on business,' Rhoda went on. 'But Humphrey doesn't care for him much.'

She straightened a dim glass oval on the wall. Ruth's eyes followed her.

'I see you are admiring my needlework pictures,' said Rhoda. Ruth, who could hardly see anything, searched her heart for words of admiration and could find none. 'The last of my mother's pieces,' said Rhoda. 'From my home in Ringwood.'

There was a slight pause.

'Mrs Wilcox,' murmured Ruth. 'Are there any arrangements for having a bath?'

Rhoda looked pensive, as if she had not reckoned on such a request.

'The only bathroom is downstairs in the flat. I suppose you could come down at six o'clock for a quarter of an hour and have a bath. But do not, I beg you, disturb Humphrey.'

Ruth walked towards the window and tried to move it.

'Does it open?' she asked Rhoda.

'I don't think so.' Rhoda's voice was remote. 'But you will be very comfortable here. I have made up the bed myself. There is an electric kettle. You have your own lavatory next door but as it is not much used Humphrey has taken to keeping some of his wine in there. Marianne will clean your room once a week: I will tell you what to pay her. And you can have your bath at six o'clock in the evenings.'

'One thing,' she added, with a minatory outstretched arm. 'We are both writers. We need peace and quiet downstairs. I hope you will not introduce any . . .' She searched for the right word. 'Distractions,' she brought out finally. Ruth knew what she meant.

She sank down on the bed in panic, not daring to move until the sound of Rhoda's heels had disappeared down the iron staircase. Then, as quietly as if she were being overheard, she crept along the corridor, down the staircase, through the kitchen and into the reassuring safety of the street.

Here all was pleasure and purpose. The sun, once more, blazed; thin dresses were still being worn, tables outside cafés were thronged, everyone was in an exceptional humour. 'L'étonnant été d'octobre', announced France-Soir on its front page, and showed a photograph of an elderly couple sunning themselves on a bench in the Tuileries. Ruth walked. Under chestnut trees now the colour of her hair, she walked all day, trying to decide whether she were better or worse off than she had been at home. On the whole, worse, she thought. As dusk fell, she wandered slowly back up the rue de Passy, admiring the shops, the bright-eyed, quick-tempered people, the beautiful children. She was now very tired and realized that she might sleep, even in that terrible room. She bought some milk and some coffee and turned into the rue des Marronniers.

That had been three weeks ago. Since then, she had got used to shutting up her books in the Bibliothèque Nationale at five sharp, so that she could clock in in time for her bath, had even got used to Humphrey observing her through a crack in the bathroom door. The evenings were long, that was the only thing. The mazy pleasures of Paris distracted her in the daytime, and besides, there was so much to do, so much work, so much French to be spoken, meals to be eaten in the *brasserie* round the corner, books to be bought. In the evenings, though, she did not always feel like reading. Bursts of foggy music from the cinema next door signalled the beginning and end of the performances; high heels tapping along the corridor announced the return home of her neighbours, whom she had never met. She felt too humble to buy a radio.

One endless Sunday she went to the Louvre. She made the classic promenade down the Champs Elysées, through the Tuileries to the Square Court, where children were wheeling about on their bicycles, and because she was reluctant to leave the still warm air, over the Pont des Arts and up the rue Bonaparte to the Luxembourg. There she sat, becalmed, going only to a café in the Place Saint-Sulpice for a sandwich some time after half past one. Dahlias blazed in the flower beds of the Luxembourg Gardens; when the gardeners removed them winter would have begun in earnest. The long straight paths were now thick with fallen leaves for it had been a very dry summer. An ancient invalid sun came out briefly to warm her iron chair but was soon vanquished by the haze obscuring the grey-blue sky. The easy days were over.

She wandered back to the Louvre, although the light was no longer good. She was indifferent to most of what she saw until she came to the Flemish primitives, with their immaculate pain and sorrow, their thoughtful grieving little heads, their chilly pallid Christs deposed, as it were, into the unhelpful climate of northern Europe. She paid a duty visit to the early-nineteenth-century galleries and was bemused, as always, by the sheer size of everything: giant figures enmeshed with one another, toiling towards rescue after shipwreck, towards liberty after oppression, towards Paris after Moscow; never would they find peace or be reconciled to their proper dimensions. At a country funeral stretching down a considerable expanse of one wall, a woman wiped her eyes with a handkerchief the size of a small tablecloth. A noble Roman, turning his back on his dead sons, twisted enormous and imperfect feet to demonstrate his anguish. In front of what she considered to be a vaguely improper allegory of Endymion being embraced by a moonbeam, she saw two youngish people convulsed with laughter. The laughter seemed to her not French; it contained the agonized excesses and repressions of English school life. She moved closer to the couple, a man and a girl. The man, though young, had white hair; the girl was dark and very pretty. They appeared to be very much in love. Their exuberance was too much for the Louvre to contain and attracted reproving looks from the attendant. As the gallery emptied and the light became bluish and obscure, Ruth and the couple found their way out and down the main staircase. She was not surprised to hear them speaking English and wished that she could signal to them that she was English herself. But she was by this time too immured in her own silence to make a sign to anyone.

They were waiting at the bus stop and had evidently wandered, as she had, back up the rue Bonaparte. She heard them discussing where to eat that evening and a great pain filled her, that she should never be able to make such plans. The impossibility of her present life was apparent to her as it had never been before. She was a prisoner in her cell, and in addition to her physical restraints she had imprisoned herself in a routine as destructive of liberty and impulse as if it had been imposed on her by a police state. Every morning she caught the same bus to the Bibliothèque Nationale. Every lunchtime she ate a sandwich in the same café. Every evening she presented herself for her bath and returned, chilly, to her room where, she was beginning to realize, problems of increased loneliness awaited her. She studied the couple closely, as if they were an unknown species. They were, in fact, an unknown species. They were happy.

In her blue dress, in which she had not taken Paris by storm, and her wool coat, Ruth felt shabby and obedient. The girl wore trousers and a pullover, the man a well-cut suit of tweed. A great desire for change came over Ruth and a great uncertainty as to how this might be brought about. For she knew, obscurely, that she had capacities as yet untried but that they might be for ever walled up unless her circumstances changed. Love, she supposed, might do it, but there was no one with whom she might fall in love. Nobody even looked at her, except Humphrey. She shuddered at the thought. At that moment the bus arrived, and in her abstracted move to board it she hit the young man's elbow with her shoulder bag.

'So sorry,' she said automatically.

He smiled. 'We thought you were English. French people take the Louvre far more seriously. Especially on a Sunday.'

They sat down facing each other. She was, in fact, unmistakably English in her heavy coat, with her heavy bag, and her heavy hair obscuring the shape of her head. Since the dinner with Richard she had ceased to pay much attention to her appearance.

'We were admiring your hair,' said the girl. 'You don't often see that colour here.'

Ruth always deprecated her hair, which seemed to her too flashy for her personality, marking her out when she found it more restful to be obscure.

'I ought to have it cut,' she replied. 'But I don't quite know where to go.'

'There's a good place next door to our flat,' said the girl. 'Rue Marboeuf. Where are you getting off?'

'At the Alma.' Ruth was quite dazed by the suddenness with which this exchange had been effected. She was also trying to take in the news that these two English people had a flat. In Paris.

'That's our stop,' the girl said. 'Why don't we have a coffee, then I can show you.'

They were called Hugh and Jill Dixon. They held each other's hands and told her about themselves. They had been married three months. Hugh was a dealer in Old Master drawings; Jill worked in a travel agency. They had each, separately, lived in Paris for some years and had met at a party. They were – and here Ruth felt a disappointment mixed with a dawning excitement – thinking of going back to London.

'If you ever want to get rid of the flat,' she murmured, 'I'd be delighted . . .'

The girl grimaced. 'There are dozens of people after it. And it's not much to look at. But you know what it's like trying to find a place here.'

Ruth found that she could make them laugh by describing her room in the rue des Marronniers, Humphrey and Rhoda, and the bathing regulations. It was a talent she had often used with Anthea; with Anthea, however, it did not always work. She was quite exhilarated by the success of her performance and insisted on paying for their coffee. It was turning into one of the best Sundays she had ever known.

They were a picturesque couple, she so dark, he so prematurely white. They had the perfect teeth and the permanent tan of the very rich, yet the girl's accent was suburban. The man was even less easy to place. He was young, immaculate, worldly, yet Ruth sensed that the last two attributes had been acquired quite recently. His watch was too expensive, his shoes, obviously handmade, too new. But above all, they were pleasant. Jill laughed a lot, as if everything amused her; sometimes she giggled for no apparent reason. The man merely smiled. He was more serious.

They took her back to the flat, which was tiny and dark but nevertheless desirable. It seemed to Ruth an ideal refuge and she began to long for it quite painfully. She repeated that she would be grateful if they would let her know if they decided to leave. She gave them her telephone number in the rue des Marronniers. It was then that she realized that she had missed her bathtime.

The look of horror on her face sent them both into peals of laughter. In her new mood of liberation Ruth felt that she had more time than usual at her disposal. She invited them out to dinner, since there was no point in going back to the rue des Marronniers until much later.

Jill and Hugh turned out to have serious appetites. They took her to a noisy restaurant which they said was quite famous and they ate their way purposefully through several courses and drank a bottle of wine. It was restful being with them. They knew where to go, what to do; they were not fearful or shy and they seemed to like her. Her knowledge of Balzac did not seem to put them off. Ruth, cautiously, began to relax.

'You don't have to go to the library every day,' said Hugh. 'First thing tomorrow, you have your hair cut. Then you meet me for lunch so that I can see what you look like.'

'Would you mind?' asked Ruth of Jill, who choked again with laughter over her coffee.

It was very late. She had never been out so late before in Paris. They took her to the Métro and thanked her for dinner, but she felt that it was she who was indebted to them. The rue des Marronniers was silent; only the concierge's dog was being walked by his owner, who wore his carpet slippers. He raised his hand silently to Ruth, acknowledging her presence for the first time since her arrival. She felt exhilarated and grateful. That night she slept without dreaming.

Under Hugh's direction Ruth had her hair cut very short and abandoned her heavy coat for a pale and expensive mackintosh in which she was never quite warm enough. She acquired pale stockings and pale shoes, but insisted on retaining her blue dress, which she had bought in such good faith in Kensington High Street. Hugh shook his head disapprovingly.

'A tartan skirt,' he said, brooking no argument. 'Think about it, Ruth.'

'Do you realize how much money I've spent?' asked Ruth, who immediately regretted what she had said. It seemed to her that money was faintly indecent, something to be dealt with in secret. Hugh had no such inhibitions. He was usually short of it himself, and quite happy to let her pay for the coffee or the lunches they would have to conclude the purchase of yet another improvement. Feeling that she was being disloyal to Jill by spending so much time with Hugh, Ruth would insist on taking them both out to dinner or to an enormous lunch that occupied most of Sunday afternoon. She found Hugh an amusing and instructive companion. His art dealing seemed to leave him an immense amount of free time, although sometimes he took her with him to a gallery, making use of her fluent French when he wanted to discuss something with the owner. He also took her to see an elderly Polish painter, of whom he had great hopes, for the same purpose. With Jill at her travel firm all day, he found Ruth useful and pleasant to be with; he was not a man to enjoy his own company.

Ruth's visits to the Bibliothèque Nationale became less regular, her knowledge of Paris more extensive. Hugh took her to Balzac's house in Auteuil, to the Musée de la Chasse, the Musée de l'Armée, to the Buttes Chaumont. He specialized in outings that were both authentic and free. He took her to antiquarian bookshops and to street markets and to a lecture by the famous Professor Duplessis at the Sorbonne. This last event was particularly impressive, for the amphitheatre was full – they had to sit in the front row – the delivery magnificent, and the students vociferous in their approval. Ruth was reminded, with a sharp pang of feeling, of the occasional beauty of academic life. Hugh also took Ruth back to her room one day and began to make love to her; she was so amazed

98

that she forgot all the routine objections.

'But *why?*' she asked.

He shrugged. 'Why not?'

There was no doubt that her looks improved. She put on weight and brushed her hair and learnt the difficult Parisian art of being immaculately turned out, although she had only one cold tap and indifferent lighting to help her. Her heels clipped along the corridor with authority these days, and she was no longer afraid of having time on her hands. The money was going pretty fast, for she could not refuse to tide Hugh over from time to time. But her work also was going fast, and at this rate of progress she should have enough money to see her through.

Hugh, she was well aware, was an adventurer. She had read about such people, and anyway he made no bones about it. He did most things for money or pleasure; if it was possible to combine the two, he did. His wife, who earned enough to pay their weekly bills, regarded him sympathetically as an agreeable and amusing accomplice. She, who had had many trips and much hospitality free from the travel agency, did not doubt that you made the most of what was offered and took it by force if necessary. If Hugh got his lunches paid for she did not grudge him the time spent with Ruth, whom she regarded as a pleasant bore.

Ruth, who knew most of this by instinct, began to think of the world in terms of Balzacian opportunism. Her insights improved. She perceived that most tales of morality were wrong, that even Charles Dickens was wrong, and that the world is not won by virtue. Eternal life, perhaps – but who knows about that? Not the world. If the moral code she had learnt, through the literature she was now beginning to reinterpret, were correct, she should surely have flourished in her heavy unbecoming coat, in her laborious solitude, with her notes and the daily bus ride and the healthful lonely walks. Yet here she was, looking really not too bad, having spent more than half her money, eating and drinking better than she had ever done in her life, and absconding from the Bibliothèque Nationale to spend time with another woman's husband. Rhoda Wilcox eyed her even more narrowly when they met in the kitchen these days. The elder Mrs Weiss would not have known what to make of her at all.

She had much to think about; that was what was so agreeable about kicking over the traces. That was what they did not tell you. It was no longer a question of whether she should or should not do such and such a thing but whether she would or would not. Yet she was aware of something out of joint. She would have preferred the books to have been right. The patient striving for virtue, the long term of trial, the ecstasy of earned reward: these things would never now be hers. She had deviated from the only path she knew and she had lost her understanding of the world before the fall. That there had been a fall, she was quite sure. She had only to look at her glowing self to be assured of that. And selfishness and greed and bad faith and extravagance had made her into this semblance of a confident and attractive woman, had performed the miracle of forcing her to grow up and deal competently with the world. People seemed to like her more this way. The concierge waved from his window to her, night and morning. There was indeed much to think about.

Late November and still dry. Ruth walked to the Bibliothèque Nationale in a cold white mist, past the American Church, to have a look at the esplanade of the Invalides in this peculiar light. Footfalls were muffled, voices enigmatic. A bus seethed past on almost silent wheels: 'Jean Nicot', sang out the conductor mournfully. Her head down, Ruth thought about Christmas, a festival celebrated with a certain amount of bad temper in the Weiss household. For the last few years George had bought a hamper from Harrods and a small cooked turkey. There never seemed to be anything practical to eat. The elder Mrs Weiss had filled the flat with the odour of a roasting goose and red cabbage, although officially she ignored the occasion of Christmas. Helen, on the other hand, became sentimentally religious, fingered her late mother's rosary, and said, 'Of course, we should have gone to church.' They never did because George was not quite sure where he stood and did not care to offend his mother while she was still alive. After Mrs Weiss's death there was Mrs Cutler who claimed to be able to say her prayers just as well in an open field as any of those sanctimonious buggers down the road. Helen, sticky with crystallized apricots, agreed with her. George spent most of the day in front of the television. Ruth either read in her room or went out for a walk.

Now, with her sharpened sense of the pleasures of life, she did not think she could return to London for just such another Christmas. She would telephone and tell them that she was going away, as indeed she planned to do in January, and that she was unwilling to interrupt her work. She would stay here, no doubt invite Hugh and Jill out for a tremendous meal, or even walk silently by herself. She was quite happy to do so.

There was an additional reason for staying in Paris. Anthea, now married to Brian, might be coming through on her honeymoon, and although Ruth could see her in London, she felt that she would like to surprise Anthea in Paris and perhaps introduce her to Hugh and Jill. It seemed to her that she had many options open to her, and she was not willing to forego any of them, not even for the week she might have spent in London, having multiple baths, unobserved.

And after these festivities, these celebrations, she would give Balzac his due. In the silent month of January she would journey west and south through France to Angers and Angoulême and Issoudun and Sancerre and

Alençon: the settings for some of Balzac's provincial novels and ground that might yield up secrets. She did not doubt that it was all changed now, prosperous and busy and emancipated, but she had an instinct, perhaps a correct one, that in the most quiet and private month of the year the small towns might regress to their former innocent complexity, and that she might learn something of the intricacies of provincial life in the early years of the nineteenth century. She would stay in very small hotels, eat in the same restaurants every day; she would train her ear and her eye, and eventually she might read the texts in a new and enlightened way.

She arrived later than usual at the Bibliothèque Nationale, her cheeks flushed from her long walk. The surly attendant greeted her with a faint smile, as did the man seated at the numbered place next to hers. Something about this man's appearance, his bulky figure, his air of patient stoicism, teased her memory. It was not until he put on his hat, with its brim turned up all the way round, and went out for lunch that she realized who he was: Professor Duplessis. He was back within the hour, raised his hat to her as she rose to go out in her turn. It was a disorganized day. When she took her seat again at half past two she found him deep in her copy of *La Muse du Département*.

'What are you working on?' he whispered.

'Vice and Virtue in Balzac,' Ruth whispered back.

He nodded. 'There is plenty of both. When I was much younger I wrote something on Balzac myself.'

'I know,' Ruth whispered more enthusiastically. 'I have it.'

A man with a beret, a muffler, and a thousand file cards regarded them irritably. The library settled down for the afternoon.

'I enjoyed your lecture last week so much,' said Ruth in a nearly normal voice. 'I was wondering if I might dare to ask to see you.'

'Silence!' hissed the man with the file cards.

'What time do you finish here?' asked Professor Duplessis. 'I must leave at five sharp today. Can you spare the time for a cup of coffee?'

Ruth smiled with pleasure. 'I should be delighted,' she said.

So at five o'clock they looked at each other and left the library, opening their briefcases for inspection at the door, and straightening in the cold white mist that blurred the street lights in the rue de Richelieu. They went to a bar and talked; Ruth was aware that he had wanted to leave for somewhere at five sharp but he seemed to have forgotten. No man had ever asked her so many questions. Where did she live? Were her parents alive? How long would she stay in Paris? Which way did she intend to walk home? Did she always walk home?

'I don't think I shall tonight,' said Ruth, aware that she had missed her bath again.

'Then allow me to drive you home,' said Professor Duplessis.

They met the following day, and the day after that. Then the weekend intervened and she had time to think about him. You cannot think about a man if he is there. With his absence grows romantic love.

Professor Duplessis was not her ideal of a romantic lover. He was about fifty, comfortable looking, rather heavy. He was watchful and patient and kind; he loved information and he dealt with it seriously. He remembered everything she told him, nodding his head over it. He would never harm her, of that she was sure. She nearly trusted him; of that too she was sure. He was neither exciting nor challenging; she did not wake up in the morning wondering how she might please him. In the days that followed, she only knew that she would feel unprotected without his neutral, faintly resigned presence, that she could not go home without his arm steering her to the neon-lit café. Still he asked her questions. Did she eat a balanced diet? Did she keep well? Would she not be safer living in an hotel? He himself lived in the rue de la Pompe, which was near La Muette, so he often took her home. She walked less, saw Hugh less. She was aware that Professor Duplessis might love her, that she might yet be redeemed.

One morning it teemed with rain and she darted out of the house in the rue des Marronniers with her hands apprehensively sheltering her newly coiffed hair. His car was waiting at the kerb. Once he walked into the *brasserie* where she ate her evening meal, made her finish it all up, and then drove her out into the Bois; they had coffee and brandy at a flashily discreet hotel with a log fire and a huge dog stretched out in front of it. Once he took her out to lunch in the Place de la Sorbonne; they trotted over a sea of cobbles to reach the restaurant and when they arrived the waiter kissed her hand. There were no other diners. For the very first time she ate lobster, forbidden on her father's side. Once she got back to her seat in the Bibliothèque Nationale and found on her papers a bunch of Parma violets, their leaves still wet, sprayed from a watering can by a flower seller in the Place de l'Opéra. She kept them for ten days.

He was married, of course. He had a wife called Noémi and two grown-up daughters. He had told her this and by mutual consent they never referred to it again.

'What can I give you,' she asked him, 'when you give me so much?'

'First you must learn to take,' he answered. And he continued to give.

As she emerged from the bathroom, Rhoda said, 'Oh, by the way, a friend of yours telephoned. Althea. Would you get in touch with her at the Hôtel Madison? I have written it on the pad. But not now, please, my dear; I

104

cannot have Humphrey disturbed. This hour before dinner is so precious to him.'

Humphrey, pen in hand, was standing watch by the telephone, his eyes fixed on Ruth's bare legs.

Anthea! She was actually here, her dearest friend. Ruth dressed, smoothed her hair, and ran out to the nearest café and the nearest telephone. Yes, Anthea was free. Of course, Ruth would come over straight away. They were longing to see one another.

But each was surprised by the other's appearance. Anthea had put on weight, looked warm and untidy in the more purposeful Parisian atmosphere. Ruth, Anthea remarked, looked almost human. She could think of no further recommendations to make. The words 'Why don't you?' died on her lips.

But there was masses to tell. Once more Ruth described her peculiar lodgings, protesting that she did not intend to stay there, that the room was cheap, that it was not too far out. Anthea gave her a withering glance.

'I'll see for myself,' she said. 'We'll take you back after dinner.'

'Dinner,' said Ruth with rather more authority than she had displayed before to Anthea, 'is on me.'

'Fine,' said Anthea, unmoved. A rush of waters from the bathroom signalled the imminent arrival of Brian.

'Are you happy?' Ruth asked directly.

Anthea hesitated for only a fraction of a second.

'Of course,' she said. 'We always suited each other. And he's got a future. Besides, I'm used to him.'

She looked at her friend, trying to reconcile her protégée of recent years with this expensive and assured looking creature in her mackintosh, her normally anxious eyes calm under her beautiful fringe.

'And what about you?' They were speaking in lowered tones. 'There's a man, I take it?'

Ruth nodded.

'At last,' said Anthea grimly. 'Well,' she added, more

as a matter of form than anything else, 'did the earth move?'

Ruth did not even blush, as she would have done before.

'Oh yes,' she replied. 'Yes, it did.'

Anthea's eyes widened. 'Now, for God's sake, Ruth, don't make a mess of this. Don't give in too easily. String him along. Keep him guessing. Break the odd appointment. How do you think I got Brian after all these years?'

Ruth looked sadly at her friend.

'Is it all a game, then?' she asked.

Anthea looked sadly back. 'Only if you win,' was her reply. 'If you lose, it's far more serious.'

13

George, much to his annoyance, seemed to be going deaf in one ear. He went down to the doctor's surgery, thinking to have some wax removed, but was met with a kind of hearty complicity he did not greatly appreciate.

'Nothing to be done,' said Dr Maxwell. 'One of the penalties of getting on a bit.' He never spoke of growing old and always pretended to be the same age as the patient he was treating.

Nevertheless, George was put out. Getting on a bit? He was no age at all, and twice the man he had been a mere two years ago. From five to six thirty every evening he took his ease in Sally's flat, which he also liked to think of as his flat. 'Let's go back to the flat,' he would say. She would cook him a little something and enjoin him to relax, as if he had performed some immense labour. The shop was left increasingly in the care of Mrs Jacobs's sister's boy, Roddy, who was waiting to hear if he had got a job at Sotheby's and who would otherwise have been working as an assistant at Harrods. The arrangement pleased everyone concerned.

In Bayswater George rediscovered the delights of his youth. Mrs Jacobs behaved just like his mother. 'You look tired,' she would say. 'You do far too much.' His towelling bathrobe hung next to her own and a variety of lotions and powders had pride of place in her hitherto unsullied bathroom. Signs of his presence, actual or intended, were everywhere to be seen. In the teeth of Mrs

Jacobs's protests he had rigged up a machine for making morning tea by the side of her bed. The only time she had used it, steam had squirted out sideways, damaging the valance of her satin counterpane. Some of the furniture in the sitting room was placed on the slant because of the size of the speakers from the record player. George's sun lamp was in the spare room and his portable grill was in the kitchen. Sally had put her foot down when she had seen him plugging it in, although the corners of her mouth had only seemed to contract with disappointment as the other items were introduced. George had taken no notice. But, 'I do all the cooking that goes on here,' she said. 'You can take that back and get a credit note.' But George had never got around to it somehow.

The delights of his youth. A little bit of smoked fish as an appetizer. Cold meat loaf and horseradish. Cucumbers in sour cream. And cheesecake, which Sally made herself, and which was so rich that he had to eat it with a spoon. And all the while he ate she would sit at the table and watch him sternly, her face propped in her hand, to see that he left nothing on his plate.

She loved to have a man to feed again. The disruption of her flat, the intrusion of all the devices, which she never used, seemed a small price to pay for the pleasure of seeing George every evening. When the time came for him to leave, she would brush his collar and become slightly tearful. It was not that she desired any further physical contact; she just hated to go to bed uncomforted.

'Couldn't you at least telephone me to say goodnight?' she sniffed as George prepared to revert to his real life in Oakwood Court and she was faced with the washing up and the preparation of the next evening's snack.

'Well, darling, it's a bit difficult. I suppose I could take the telephone into another room but I'd hate Helen to get wind of anything.

Mrs Jacobs sniffed harder. 'If you really loved me,

you'd try,' she murmured.

So every evening, by dint of sending Mrs Cutler in with a hot milk drink which Helen barely touched, and by turning up the volume of the television very loud, he telephoned Mrs Jacobs to say goodnight.

'Where were you just now?' asked Helen one evening.

'Ringing Mrs Jacobs about an order,' said George, quite truthfully.

'That woman doesn't seem to be able to do anything on her own,' said Helen, shaking her sleeping pills out of the bottle.

'We find it works better if I ring her up in the evening to remind her what to expect the next day,' said George, half terrified at his own daring.

'Silly bitch,' sighed Helen, closing her pale blue eyelids. 'She must be losing money hand over fist.' Her eyes snapped open again. 'Make sure she pays you properly,' she admonished George. She was being quite serious.

George was delighted. By dint of beginning his conversation very heartily and modulating it to a dying fall, he found that he was almost telling the truth to Helen and pleasing Sally as well. He liked to think of Sally sitting up in bed in her expensive nightdress, her special little pillow behind her neck, her satin curtains (five hundred pounds, she had told him, and she had sent them back twice) pulled fast against the night. Reality awaited him next door where Helen prepared to retire by brushing the crumbs off her cardigan, removing her denim cap and slinging it into a corner, and placing her book face down, spine cracking, on the cluttered bedside table. After getting into bed beside her, George reflected on the virtue of his behaviour. No sin, no *act* had been committed. He remained a faithful husband, didn't he? Sally loved him. And he was eating better than he had for years.

So that when Dr Maxwell told him that he was getting on a bit he was disagreeably surprised.

'It's my wife you really want to take a look at,' he protested. 'She hardly ever gets out of bed these days. And she never goes out.'

He had a reason for wanting to re-animate Helen apart from the uneasiness he felt when he saw her stick-like arms and legs. If Helen rose from her bed and somehow, miraculously, recovered her command, he could get rid of Mrs Cutler and find someone slightly more menial. And he wanted to do this because he had an idea that Mrs Cutler knew what he was up to. Technical innocence would be no weapon to withstand Mrs Cutler's condemnation. And she would make a point of telling Helen, who would make scenes and take more sleeping pills, simply because she had been given her cue. It was not to be contemplated.

Dr Maxwell looked grave. 'That of course is much more serious. Her circulation will begin to suffer very soon. Is her mind all right?'

George shrugged. Had Helen's mind ever been all right? She had always been a mythomaniac, fascinated by her own legend, recounting it to everyone. To think of the years he had spent just listening to her. But of course he could not leave her now. He stirred uncomfortably. He wished he had not come to the doctor in the first place if he was just going to be made more depressed about everything. His ear, Helen's circulation, Sally's loneliness, which he did not take very seriously. Mrs Cutler's watchful eye. With an effort he concentrated on what the doctor was saying. Helen's mind?

'Yes, her mind's all right,' he replied. 'She reads most of the time. Our housekeeper sees that she eats a bit. Not much, you know. Snacks. Perhaps you could give her a vitamin injection or something?'

He looked and felt suddenly helpless.

'Of course,' he added, 'if this goes on much longer I may have to send for my daughter.'

He wished that he had not thought of that. But on

110

reflection, it might settle things all round.

Helen herself was in a curious state of mind, sometimes invalidish, sometimes masterful. She felt that she was saving herself for some tremendous come-back, would be discovered, behind closed doors, for the part of a lifetime. At the same time she was dimly aware that her energy had run out in some irreversible fashion which she could not identify. She was almost glad to regress, spending the days in her nightgown, looking like a haggard girl. 'The rest is doing me good,' she maintained, but they could not see what had made her so tired. She was still beautiful, still cleverly made up, although her hair was now long and untidy. She had altered in the sense that she now demanded to be amused rather than to dominate the conversation with anecdotes of her former fame or some screamingly funny incident that had taken place when they were on tour. Helen read a novel a day, preferring those that she had read before, and twice a week Mrs Cutler had to set out with her wheeled trolley for the public library to bring home six nearly identical stories. These had to do with maidens in the nineteenth century, taking posts as governesses and losing their hearts to the rakish son who was also the black sheep of the family. Helen, her blue eyes dreamy in their huge sockets, murmured, 'They never go to bed with them. I wonder if that's where I went wrong.' Mrs Cutler said nothing. It disgusted her that Helen should still be thinking about sex. She had got over that sort of thing herself.

But it was in fact Mrs Cutler who was bringing the matter to life again. Mrs Cutler had made an unexpected hit at the Hazel Kilpatrick Introductions Agency, which operated from a small room up a flight of stairs off Kensington High Street. Hazel Kilpatrick herself, a retired social worker, took the application more seriously than Mrs Cutler had done. Grimly parting with a fee of ten pounds, Mrs Cutler had decided to let her get on with it. So far, five answers to her application had been received. Helen bestirred herself to patter to the door every morning to collect the post, which she ripped open and then spread all over the bed. 'I like the sound of this one,' she would say to the resigned Mrs Cutler who now, in addition to doing her own chestnut lights, had to do Helen's as well. 'Recently retired,' she read out. 'That means he's knocking on seventy. Just about right for you, Maggie.' Mrs Cutler thought seventy was too old. Helen, who when she thought about it found most men too old these days, reprimanded her. 'There's no point in being starry-eyed about this sort of thing. It's not as if you were in it for a roll in the hay.' Mrs Cutler winced. George, who had put his head round to door to say goodbye, also winced. Helen's language was getting coarser. She sometimes referred off-handedly to the financial habits of Jews. George found this unmannerly and said so. There had been several unharmonious evenings, complicated by the consumption of a little too much whisky. Mrs Cutler, her head throbbing the following morning, vowed that it could not go on; she might have to get married after all. George, seeing both women equally afflicted, hoped that they had learnt their lesson and went off virtuously to Mount Street, where Jews were never mentioned and liquor never consumed.

It could not in fact go on. Mrs Cutler retrieved the papers of Leslie Arthur Dunlop, recently retired, from Helen's bed, and wrote secretly to him, arranging a meeting at the Mexicana coffee bar. He turned out to be a cheery elderly man, very spruce and clearly very lonely. He had thin sleeked-back pepper and salt hair and he wore a blazer with the insignia of what Mrs Cutler thought was his regiment on the pocket. He had come up from Folkestone, where he had a bungalow, for the day. The Mexicana was just about his mark. Mrs Cutler wore her jade green coat and skirt, a silk blouse abstracted from Helen's wardrobe, sling-back court shoes which were

112

murder after half an hour, and her pearl earrings. She was careful not to smoke too much or even to say too much until it became clear that Leslie Arthur Dunlop wanted to light his pipe. Hesitantly, she suggested that they go next door to the Black Lion; he cheered up immediately. He ordered a pint of beer and she had a vodka and lime. His good humour reminded her of George but she reserved judgment. After the pub he took her out for a Chinese meal, which neither of them enjoyed. 'Wait till you taste my cooking,' said Mrs Cutler imprudently, 'you won't know you're born.' Mr Dunlop cheered up even further. 'My late wife wasn't much of a cook,' he reminisced, 'but she kept a lovely home.' 'I do that too,' said Mrs Cutler.

'That agency seems to have given you up as a bad job,' said Helen in disgust, as nothing further came through the post. 'They probably think you're too old.'

Mrs Cutler, who was meeting Mr Dunlop again on her next afternoon off – they were going to the first house at the Palladium – did not reply. Better to let them think what they liked. What she did was her own affair. She had reapplied her chestnut lights and varnished her nails: she held them out from her stiffly while they dried. Then, with exaggerated distaste, she removed the bottle of whisky from its resting place on Helen's bedside table and made a shepherd's pie for lunch.

'You're going to eat this whether you like it or not,' she shouted from the kitchen. 'You've got as thin as a rake.' She was a little uneasy about Helen who seemed to take a delight in making herself helpless these days. She would totter to the bathroom, but would not take a bath on her own. Mrs Cutler, pressed into service, did not like the look of her white knobbly spine curved over into an old woman's position, her fleshless arms, her narrow unused feet. With a gesture unconsciously retained from earlier days, Helen held a towel to her disappearing bosom as she stepped unsteadily out of the bath. Her shoulders were still good, her face beautiful, but so pale, so lined until she had reapplied her make-up: the face of a beautiful old woman.

Mrs Cutler, whose initial attachment to Leslie Arthur Dunlop was as a pretext for leaving Oakwood Court, had developed a rather more reasoned liking for the man when he insisted on calling her Margaret. She in turn called him Leslie, although he had always been known as Les, he said. That was what his first wife had called him. 'Not me,' said Mrs Cutler. There was a moment's silence while each digested this exchange. Had they committed themselves? They looked at each other. It seemed as though they had. 'We can't live on your pension,' said Mrs Cutler, her cheeks highly coloured by rouge and emotion. 'We'll have to get a job somewhere. Living in, so that we can let the bungalow. What about one of those old people's homes? You can save all your wages there.'

'Here, here,' protested Leslie, fending her off humorously with his pipe. He was not quite so spruce this time. 'What about all that home cooking you were telling me about?'

'Plenty of time for that,' said Mrs Cutler (Margaret as she now thought of herself). 'First things first.' She saw herself in the Lurex two-piece she had bought in the sales, being absolutely charming to some old dear while her husband hovered cheerily in the background. 'My husband will take care of it,' she would say. 'You will have to speak to my husband about that.' They would make an ideal pair. After all, if she could look after Helen, she could look after a few more. And they had nurses, didn't they? She sent Leslie back to Folkestone with instructions to make enquiries at all likely establishments along the coast. Then she nipped back to the Black Lion and had two gins to steady her nerves after her momentous afternoon.

14

'Do you realize,' said George to Mrs Jacobs, 'that if you didn't feed me, I'd never get anything to eat?'

They were washing up together in the immaculate kitchen, after listening to the obligatory Viennese waltz on the record player. Mrs Jacobs shook her head sadly. George was now nearly a stone overweight. Mrs Jacobs, on the other hand, was thinner and less happy than she had been. George kept her in in the evenings and she had had to abandon her bridge friends. She loved cooking for him – she had even made him a pound of coconut biscuits to keep in the car – but she thought she was a bit ill-used. And he had failed to show compunction over the ruined counterpane. And her nephew Roddy was beginning to hint that she might make him a partner in the shop as he was doing most of the work. All in all, Mrs Jacobs felt, George ought to marry her. That was the conclusion at which she had arrived in the small hours of that morning. Once they were married, she could go out again. She was thinking in terms of a cruise, when George made his significant statement about lack of food.

They took their lemon tea back to the sitting room. Mrs Jacobs massaged cream into her hands and slipped her rings back on. George glanced at his watch, belched very softly, and told himself he would not be sorry to get to bed. Leading a double life could prove tiring. He held out his hand to Mrs Jacobs with a charming impulsive smile. Had she but known it, this was how he used to behave with Helen, when they had temporarily run out of sex or conversation. Mrs Jacobs took his hand and smiled herself. It was for moments like these that she endured the knowledge that George still lived with his wife, a knowledge that compounded her own loneliness. She often urged him to spend more time in Bayswater, to stroll along on a Sunday morning and stay for an early lunch, but he refused. At least she had got him to telephone her every night. That call was necessary to her. Without it she doubted if she could go on facing the troubled dreams with which she was afflicted, and the unnecessary spaces of her large double bed.

It was time to leave. George gave his usual sigh, straightened his cuffs, and heaved himself out of Mrs Jacobs's husband's favourite chair, while Mrs Jacobs stood beside him like an acolyte. When he had gone she would plump up the cushions, leave instructions for the cleaning woman on the pad in the kitchen, and change into a housecoat. She would switch on the radio, switch if off again, make herself a last cup of tea, have her bath and take her place in the bed, waiting for George's goodnight call. An occasional flash of common sense told her that she would be better off with someone else, as her sister frequently reminded her, the news of her attachment having spread to the family via Roddy. Yet she rather loved George and they had so much in common. When he called she felt warm and tearful and anxious to prolong the conversation even though she knew that he was crouched in the drawing room with his ear blocked against the noise from the television. Sometimes she got his deaf ear and nothing much ensued. But he always said, 'Goodnight, my darling, sleep well,' and that kept her going. Well, that is to say, it kept her going until the next time.

There was one terrible evening when she did not hear from him. She rang the engineer to see if her number were in order, then contemplated ringing Oakwood

116

Court, but she knew that she must not do that. She arrived at the shop the following morning pale and trembling and had to send Roddy out to renew her prescription for tranquillizers, although George had forbidden her to take them. He liked being masterful in these little ways and she liked it too, although she usually kept an emergency supply handy. At eleven o'clock George turned up looking no less pale and sank into a chair with his head in his hands. Fearfully, Mrs Jacobs placed a glass of tea at his elbow.

'I knew it,' he said finally. 'I knew it would come to this.'

'You mean . . .' Mrs Jacobs's throat was dry. 'You mean she knows, about us?'

George raised his head from his hands and looked at her as if he could hardly remember who she was.

'I mean,' he said, 'that my bloody housekeeper is leaving. Getting married, if you please. To a chap in Folkestone. Folkestone,' he repeated, as if that last detail were the crowning insult.

Mrs Jacobs was bewildered.

'But you never liked her. You always said she was no good.'

George sipped his tea grimly. 'That's hardly the point now,' he told her. 'She's been with us for years. Looks after Helen. Knows all her little ways. Nobody else is likely to take her on.'

'Why ever not?' asked Mrs Jacobs. She only knew of Helen as charming, spoilt, beautiful, selfish, and lazy; she did not know of the long straggling hair, the nightdress stained with coffee, the horny fingernails under the chipped polish. George tried to tell her.

'But she's no age at all,' cried Mrs Jacobs in surprise. 'You must put your foot down. She's not old and incapable. If you don't watch out you'll have an invalid on your hands.'

George, who had had just that for several months now

117

– ever since their holiday, in fact, and the last time Helen
had been out – said nothing.

'I'll find you another housekeeper,' urged Mrs Jacobs.
'I'll put an advertisement in the *Lady*. I'll interview her
for you. All I ask is that you don't interrupt our routine.'
She burst into tears. 'I can't go back to the doctor again
and that's what it would do to me.'

George rubbed his hands unhappily. 'I don't want to
interrupt anything, darling.' He had visions of himself
being tied to the house, doing the cooking, the cleaning,
and, worst of all, listening to Helen all day.

'What about your daughter?' said Mrs Jacobs. 'When is
she due home?'

George raised his head and calculated. 'What is it now?
March? She's due back in the summer, I believe. At least,
that was the original plan. As you know, I was against
her going.'

They looked at each other. 'Well,' said Mrs Jacobs. 'I
think that's the answer, don't you?'

Mrs Cutler, to her surprise, had not looked forward to
telling Helen that she was leaving, so she had told George
first. His reaction was one of total amazement and blank
outrage.

'Married?' he echoed. 'Married?'

'I told you I had it in mind when you came back from
Brighton,' she said with eyes downcast, like a maiden in
one of Helen's novels. 'Just before Ruth went.'

'But you can't mean it,' George protested. 'We can't
do without you. And anyway, you've been married
once. Why go through it all again? If it's a question of
money . . .' he added.

Mrs Cutler recovered her dignity. She had in fact
saved one hundred pounds out of the housekeeping and
had prudently put it in a Post Office Savings Account.
Well, there was precious little housekeeping at Oakwood
Court these days, and nobody seemed to eat much, so

she bought less. No point in throwing money down the drain.

'Mr Dunlop and I have more than enough,' she replied. 'And we shall be taking another post. I am willing to stay until matters are settled. In the meantime you can look around for someone else.' Though who, she said to herself, is going to put up with this lot I fail to imagine. Still, that's their worry.

While George, a vein beating ominously in his forehead, wrenched his car in the direction of Mount Street, Mrs Cutler made herself a cup of instant coffee and sat down to think things over. The die was cast now, but she felt no enthusiasm. She looked round the big kitchen, not noticing the smell of cheese kept a little too long, or the strands of greasy fluff around the feet of the gas cooker, or the calendar, showing Constable's *Hay Wain*, which had not been changed since February. To exchange this for a bungalow in Folkestone was a gamble. But we shan't be there, she reminded herself. We shall have our own quarters in a proper house somewhere. I shan't have to wear a uniform or anything; in fact I can dress up a bit. Might get myself a couple of trouser suits. No more overalls, thank God. And he'll be easy enough to manage. A woman's no good on her own, even at my age. Margaret Dunlop, she said to herself. Sounds quite nice.

Helen, fully made up but a bit dingy about the neck, was reading. She had got to the part where the governess, maddened by despair at the rakish ne'er-do-well younger son's forthcoming engagement to the neighbouring squire's daughter, has rushed out into the night and is about to be discovered sobbing on the moor. Helen knew what was coming. Deserting the glittering lights of the ballroom, the ne'er-do-well, his black curls streaming in the wind, finds a tiny fragile figure all but spent with exhaustion. Cradling her roughly in his arms, he realizes that she is his own true love. The book jacket showed the deserted fiancée, in vast crinoline, staring in agony through the window, with a dancing couple and a chandelier in the background. Helen had read it before. Only a month before, in fact, but Mrs Cutler had other things on her mind these days and did not spend too much time at the library.

As Mrs Cutler, rakish and defiant, stepped in and started dusting the borders of various surfaces to give herself something to do, Helen sighed unconsciously as the door of the ballroom opened on to the stormy night. Why had nobody ever done as much for her? Well, nobody had had to, really, to be perfectly fair. But if only they had *tried*. If only they had *offered*. If only they had made the *slightest effort*. My God, I'm bored, she thought. If only there were something to get up for. She said as much to Mrs Cutler, who sniffed unsympathetically.

'These things don't happen in real life,' she said, thinking of Leslie's pipe and his cardigan and his darts team. 'You should know that by now.'

She was angry with Helen because in a way she saw her point. But she could not change her position now. It was too late to think again.

'By the way,' she said, her head averted. 'You'll have to find someone else to look after the place soon. I'm getting married.' She rubbed furiously at the dressing table. She felt absurdly unhappy.

Helen raised her head from her book, marked a full five seconds' pause, and raised the back of her hand to her forehead.

'You can't be,' she pronounced finally. 'The agency couldn't find anyone suitable. At least, that's what you said.'

She laid her book down, as if it were of no further use to her. Reality had taken over with its usual vengeful effect. She had always felt like this when she came off stage. And now she was never on . . . Her heart beat uncomfortably and her eyes stung with tears.

'I met him at the library,' said Mrs Cutler, hoping to

120

salvage a little good will. Helen looked so stricken that she felt a pang of remorse. Poor cow, she thought. She won't have anyone to talk to now. 'He's retiring to Folkestone,' she continued. 'He wants me to go with him.'

'Are you telling me the truth?' asked Helen, her voice gaining its old resonance. 'What's his name?'

'Arthur Godwin,' replied Mrs Cutler quickly. She wondered why she had started all this. With a shaking hand Helen lit a cigarette from the stub of her old one and ran her fine grubby fingers through her hair. A rich smell of unaired bedclothes, like humus, filled the room. In sudden disgust, Mrs Cutler shoved open the window.

Helen, after giving the matter some thought, chose to be dignified. 'You are old enough to know what you are doing,' she said, 'although for the life of me I cannot see that it is going to work. The idea of a woman of your age . . . But perhaps it is better all round.' She viewed Mrs Cutler with distaste, although only half an hour ago she had flung out a hand in one of her old flamboyant gestures. 'How soon,' she said carelessly, 'will be you leaving?'

As Mrs Cutler understood it, she was being dismissed. And she had only come in to give in her notice. She was furious to discover that her eyes were smarting. It was 'Darling Maggie' this morning, she thought, adding to herself those useless words, after all I've done for her. Wait till she asks the next one to cut her toenails or wash her back or dye her hair. And what about him? What does he get up to all day? Why doesn't he ever want to eat much in the evenings? There's a lot going on here I could say something about. But I'll rise above it. I won't go down to her level. She banged with unnecessary violence at a cushion and prepared to withdraw.

'I shan't need any lunch today,' said Helen, remote. 'But I can't get interested in this book. Perhaps you could find your way to the library this afternoon. Perhaps Mr

Godwin would be kind enough to allow you to find me something to read.'

Mrs Cutler wondered what she was talking about, then realized that she had lied instinctively to protect the married name of Dunlop. You never knew with her. But she could not quite remember whether she had mentioned Leslie's real name to George. If she had, she was in for it this evening when he came home. Helen was quite obviously working herself up to a scene, and something of her old expression was returning: that air of indomitable vitality that George called her Joan of Arc look and that had seen her through many a first night. But Mrs Cutler noticed the still shaking hands and resigned herself to losing this round.

'Fancy a cup of tea?' she conceded. 'Won't take a minute.'

George and Mrs Jacobs had taken themselves out to lunch to celebrate the imminent solution to their problem. With Ruth at home to look after her mother, there was no reason, so far as Mrs Jacobs could see, why George and she should not get married. George moved a little uneasily. He had not gone quite so far himself. He would prefer a rather longer period of time in which to toy with the possibility.

They were in a sentimental mood when they got back to Mount Street and Mrs Jacobs had to remind George quite forcibly that he should telephone Ruth without allowing any more delay. With some difficulty he found the number at which he used to contact Humphrey Wilcox. Humphrey, disturbed in mid-sentence, was not pleased to hear from him.

'She's not here any more,' he said testily. 'She's gone somewhere else.'

The vein in George's forehead began to stand out again. Mrs Jacobs put a hand on his arm. Humphrey was still complaining down the telephone. Once disturbed, he saw no reason why other people shouldn't be.

'But where is she?' George broke in.

'I can't remember,' said Humphrey, who left these matters to Rhoda. 'You'll have to ring back when Rhoda's in. Rhoda wrote it down somewhere.' In fact Ruth's new telephone number was on the pad by the telephone. But that was not Humphrey's business.

After false assurances of cordiality, they rang off. Mrs Jacobs looked determined.

'You'll have to get through again tonight,' she said. 'In fact Helen will want you to.'

Then, since things seemed to be going to pieces all round, they waited until Roddy returned from lunch and went back to Bayswater.

15

For once, Helen was impatient for George to get home. She had brushed her hair, poured herself a drink, and put on her bracelets and her wedding ring. Mrs Cutler was in voluntary exile in the kitchen. The two women had not spoken all the afternoon. The cup of tea that Mrs Cutler had taken in was clouded and untouched.

George, aware of tensions, sighed inwardly at the prospect of having to sort them out. It had been one of those unsettling spring days that induce bad temper: sudden spurts of rain alternating with ten minutes of hectic sunlight, the whole thing dissolved by rapidly moving cloud. He had eaten too much, spent too much, and he wanted to be alone. He was never alone these days. Sometimes he wished that he had never sold the shop. He had thought he was keeping up quite well with changing times, but suddenly they seemed to have changed without him.

Helen's voice hailed him as soon as he was inside the door. Wearily he went into the bedroom and beheld his wife, wreathed in smoke, but otherwise restored to some kind of competence.

'We have been deceived,' said Helen, in a resonant voice.

George nodded. Helen drained her glass.

'While I thought she was at the library, she was fixing up her future. Planning to get away. Sneaking out to meet someone. Leaving me lying here,' she said, but it didn't sound right so she abandoned that line.

'Yes,' said George. 'I wonder why we didn't hear a little earlier about Mr Dunlop.

'No, darling, his name is Godwin. Dunlop was one of the men the agency sent her. I was all in favour of Dunlop.'

George sighed again. 'It was a game to you. You should never have encouraged her. And his name is Dunlop. He lives in Folkestone.'

Helen's outrage was profound. She who had never been upstaged! Her heart beating uncomfortably fast, she poured herself another drink and drained it. After a short pause she uttered a fierce little laugh. 'They were right when they said how sharper than a servant's tooth is man's ingratitude.'

'Serpent's,' corrected George. He was very tired.

'My version is better,' said Helen. 'Well, we had better get Ruth home, I suppose.'

'That might be difficult. I tried her this afternoon, but she seems to have moved.'

'Nonsense, let me try.'

George plugged the telephone in by the bed. He would not be able to call Sally tonight, that much was clear.

'Mademoiselle,' Helen was saying to the operator, in a rich French accent assumed for the occasion. 'I am trying to get Auteuil 1047. *C'est très urgent.*'

There was but a minute's delay. '*Merci,*' said Helen, '*vous êtes bien aimable.* Hello, Rhoda, is that you? What have you done with my naughty girl?'

Still acting, thought George. Any excuse is good enough. The real worrying is left to me. He went into the kitchen to get himself a small snack, although he had eaten at Sally's, and found Mrs Cutler sitting miserably at the table with her copy of *Woman's Own* unheeded in front of her. This day, more than any other, had convinced her that a woman needs a man. They turn on you the minute they can, she thought, meaning other women. I'll never put myself in such a position again. She consented to make George a cheese sandwich, glad to have something to do, and added a sprig of parsley to the plate.

'What about her?' she sniffed, jerking her head in the direction of the bedroom.

'Better make another one,' George replied. 'She's trying to get hold of Ruth.'

While they were talking the telephone rang and it was Mr Dunlop to say that he had secured the posts of manager and manageress at the Clarence Nursing Home, just outside Folkestone, to start within the month. A real bit of luck, he said. Nice little flat. Beautiful grounds. And the incontinent were sent to the local geriatric ward, so no trouble there. Mrs Cutler cheered up. 'Goodnight, love,' she said, for the benefit of Helen who was listening with an expression of immense patrician calm on her face. 'Wrap up warm. And ring me tomorrow,' she added. After that, she went to bed appeased.

'I am waiting to get through to Ruth,' said Helen. 'Apparently she has moved into a small flat somewhere. Rhoda didn't like the sound of it at all. No more do I. Well, she can move out again, that's all. She's had long enough to do as she pleases.'

'Eat your sandwich, darling. I'll just go and look at the news. Oh, I'll take the telephone next door and ring Mrs Jacobs about tomorrow.'

Turning the volume of the television up to its fullest extent, George dialled the Bayswater number. He was reeling with fatigue, his shoes hurt him, and he wanted to hear Sally's voice. It was quite clear that Helen would not rest until she had tracked Ruth down, whatever time that was. There would be little peace that night.

Helen, after having picked the cheese out of her sandwich and eaten it, realized that Mrs Cutler had failed to provide her with her usual hot milk drink, and wandered into the kitchen to see if it had been left there. On her way down the corridor she was beguiled by the sight of George's ample back crouched over the television set through the open door of the drawing room. How old he is getting, she thought. He looked heavy and vulnerable and she felt something like a surge of overpowering affection for him. How old! And his face, so red and tired. Maybe she had neglected him a little. Maybe he needed her more than she knew. Her lips curved once more in their beautiful smile and she crept forward on her bare feet towards him. As he was using his good ear for the telephone George did not immediately hear her turn down the volume, and by the time he had said, 'Good-night, my darling, sleep well', and made his usual kissing noise, the damage was done.

16

Ruth wrote down for her own edification a maxim attributed to Louis XIV: 'Do not assess the justice of a claim by the vigour with which it is pressed.' Then she closed her notebook and packed it carefully in the corner of her suitcase. All that remained to be done was to settle up with Rhoda and bid a suitably elegiac farewell to Humphrey. Then it would be time to leave the rue des Marronniers and proceed to her new quarters and her new life. The impossible had turned out to be possible. Hugh and Jill were going back to London; Jill was expecting a baby and Ruth was to have their flat.

Strange things had happened to her over the last few weeks. January had been icy and her journeys into the Balzac heartland uncomfortable. Sometimes, after spending the day alone in an unfamiliar town, she would sit in a café, with a cup of coffee in front of her, attracting attention from the bar because a solitary woman was an unusual sight and because such Parisian looseness was not customary; sometimes she was asked rather insistently for her money. She stayed in small hotels which seemed to have no other guests, and wandered about in the fine mist, trying to kill the day, living a reduced life, speaking to no one. The evenings were a problem which she solved, or perhaps failed to solve, by going to bed very early and reading her Balzac. She fell into a heavy sleep quite soon and sometimes in the morning she would find her book on the floor.

Once, as she leaned over the parapet bordering a river, a strange man spoke to her. She did not understand what he was saying until she realized that he was deaf and dumb. In his desire to make her hear he gesticulated violently, his arms jerking up and down in their shiny blue sleeves, Frightened, she went into a church and made for a small chapel which contained a statue of the Virgin; all around were dedicatory plaques, and her eye fell on one which read, '*Notre Dame la Grande, fais que j'entende*'. After having spoken to no one for so long, she began to feel that she herself had been cut off from the realm of speech. She made her way back to the river. The man was gone, the white mist thicker. Her uneasiness deepened and she decided to go back to Paris.

Waiting at the station, she thought of Duplessis and wondered how she might get in touch with him to let him know that she was back. She could of course see him on those days when he worked at the Bibliothèque Nationale; in fact there was no other way of seeing him. The chill of the weather, her numbness and dumbness, induced a great and sudden despair. She was alone, in Angers, as it happened, although it could have been Sancerre or Alençon or Saumur, waiting on a platform for an inconvenient train; she was going back to a small dark room, and she must make her way to a public place for a chance of seeing the man who was her only source of real emotion. She, who must wait on accident, could not otherwise arrange to meet him. For all their closeness, they were denied intimacy: cafés, libraries, museums were the only places where they could be together, and she must always wait for a telephone call, for she could not telephone him, even at his office at the Sorbonne. It seemed to her that they could not continue like this, or rather that she could not. For her recent experience of spending the silent days in alien streets, of eating alone, of sleeping too much, had shaken her rather than confirmed her in her elected life. To escape from disorder into a discipline was not enough. Now she wanted an escape from the discipline into something sweeter.

If only she could sit with him in a room, quietly, talking. If only she could wait for him in some place of her own, hear his footsteps approaching. If she could cook for him, make him comfortable, make him laugh. More than that, she knew, she could not expect. Can anyone? She still measured her efforts and her experience against her disastrous failure with Richard, remembering her expectations and the reality that had destroyed them. That reality had made her wary. Disappointment was now built into any hope she might have had left. But so far Duplessis had not disappointed her.

Rain began to fall and she was glad when the train approached. Not so glad to find that it was full, mostly of young soldiers, their thick graceless uniforms and heavy boots still constructed for the trenches of the First World War. She sat unhappily on the edge of her seat, trying not to breathe in the exhaled breath of her neighbours, both asleep, their heads lolling with the motion of the train and sometimes coming to rest on her shoulders. Those who were not asleep yawned uninhibitedly. Steam whitened the windows. During the long journey her features again became blurred with the anxiety that she had laid aside a few months previously. Her hair needed cutting and she was back in her heavy coat. She felt unkempt, furtive, and without a future. All she could calculate was that her money would soon run out and that she would have to return to London. This, however, was so much of a last resort that she refused to give it any serious thought.

Montparnasse. As she struggled along the platform, the soldiers jostling all around her, her suitcase banging against her leg, she thought that she might even be glad to see Rhoda and Humphrey again. Certainly, in her present state, she could face no one else. It was mid-

February and dark, the time of year she found most difficult. Tonight the lumpy double bed of the rue des Marronniers. Tomorrow the singing radiators of the Bibliothèque Nationale. But first a bath, even if it did mean Humphrey and his little games. Through the taxi windows, each street light was blurred into a nimbus by the damp. She had a feeling that it was the middle of the night, although it was barely half past five. Once in her own room she sank for a moment on to the bed, feeling waterlogged and weak-eyed, then sighed, and picked up her towel, and went downstairs.

In the bathroom she found messages from Rhoda, propped up against the taps. 'Professor Duplessis telephoned. Hugh Dixon telephoned. Urgent.' And there was a letter, in a tiny handwriting she did not know. She looked for a signature. 'Love, Richard.' She sat down on the edge of the bath, trembling. Could this still happen? Could this abortive, unfinished business disturb her so profoundly? Would she always react in the same way to those who did not want her, trying ever more hopelessly to please, while others, better disposed, went off unregarded? She read the letter. He was sorry not to have been in touch earlier, but she would understand how busy he had been. And on top of everything, he was getting married. Did she remember Joanna? Maybe not. Anyway, there it was; he was blissfully happy and he hoped that she was too. The cheque had been most useful and he was happy to return her loan at last. He hoped she would have dinner with them both when she got back to London.

Slowly, she bent down and retrieved the cheque from the floor. Slowly, she put it in her bag. She must be sensible about this. The extra money had come just in time. She would be able to stay a little longer. That was the whole point: the money. She would have her hair done in the morning, call Hugh, see Duplessis. She would take up where she had left off. Yet she felt nothing but a burning dismay as the image of Richard's wedding bit into her. Again she thought of Phèdre. '*Hippolyte est sensible et ne sent rien pour moi*'. Lucky Joanna, whoever she was. She did not doubt that they would be happy. She crept upstairs to her room, diminished. During the evening she read the letter several times, and wept for a moment before she fell asleep.

The following weeks were a little hesitant, a little unenthusiastic. The routine resumed. She took Hugh and Jill out for lunch on Sundays, but Jill was feeling unwell and could not eat much. Hugh supervised her appearance until she was presentable again. And Duplessis was there. Gradually things returned to normal. Her pile of notes was now so thick that she decided to begin writing and in writing found some measure of equilibrium. Bright is the ring of words. She would write all day, and at five o'clock Duplessis would come for her and take her out and sit with her and then drive her home.

But as the light strengthened and the days grew longer she began to walk again, feeling a restlessness and a desire for change that she could not, within the terms of her own existence, justify. On her birthday, otherwise unrecorded, cards came from George – with a message scribbled by Helen – from Mrs Cutler, and from Anthea: 'Pregnant! Just my luck!' Ruth lost some of the weight she had put on, and walked more fiercely. After her evening meal, she would go over her notes, under the weak bulb in the jelly-mould shade judged adequate by Rhoda for a virgin scholar. She had less time for Hugh and his excursions, unwilling as she was to leave the library where she wrote and waited to be found. Her industry and application gained her the respect of the custodians and the man at the desk. She thought this might go on for ever, and sometimes hoped that it might. She was twenty-two years old.

One evening Hugh, downcast and in need of nourish-

132

ment and encouragement, appeared in the rue des Marronniers.

'Where's Jill?' asked Ruth.

'Being sick at home,' he replied. 'I think she's going to
have a baby.'

'But that's marvellous!' She hesitated. 'Aren't you
pleased?'

He sat down on her bed. 'If it's mine,' he said.

She was astounded. 'But of course it's yours! Jill adores
you.'

He shook his head. 'There's usually another man
around. She's always been the same. So beautiful, you
see.' Ruth saw. 'And normally it doesn't matter. Now it
does. I want a child. She doesn't.'

Ruth looked at him, sitting like a convict with his head
in his hands, his normally bluff face creased with misery.
She sat down beside him and put her arm around him.

'It's yours, I'm sure it's yours. And if it isn't, I don't
think you should care so much. You will be its father.
And when you see it and it looks like you, it will be an
added bonus.'

They were both silent, in the dingy room.

She thought, it doesn't matter who the father is. The
purpose has been served. You are no longer important.
Even her importance will soon be diminished. But she
said nothing, pretending not to notice his distress, not
recognizing her own. They sat together, side by side,
warily. She could hear the seconds ticking by on his
watch. Then he gave a great sigh and polished his face
with his handkerchief.

'We might as well eat, I suppose,' he said.

The immediate pleasure of the food restored him, as it
always did. That was his main attraction, his supreme
enjoyment of life. She watched him as he severed his
steak, refilled his glass. By the time he lit his cheroot he
was quite revived.

'If we go ahead with it,' he pronounced, 'we'd be

better off in London. Jill's family lives there and I imagine they'll be quite keen.'

Warmth suddenly surged into Ruth's face.

'Hugh,' she murmured, hardly daring to hope, 'can I have the flat?'

'Why not? Of course, I can't really say; it's in Jill's name. She lived there before we got married. And I suppose we'd want a nominal sum as repayment for what she had to put down to get it. You know what a business it is to get a flat here.'

Ruth thought of Richard's cheque.

'Would a hundred pounds be enough?' she asked. Her eyes were bright and beseeching, her pretty hair disarranged. Hugh looked at her and thought of his beautiful wife, of whom he had such doubts. Ruth, in so many and such surprising ways the better woman, would not measure up, he thought. In that moment he threw in his lot with Jill and the baby she would have. He could not do without her. But he smiled kindly at Ruth, grateful to her for making up his mind.

'Of course it would,' he said. 'It will take us a couple of weeks to get things arranged. Can you wait?'

A flat of her own. In the rue Marboeuf. She could work at home and cook her own meals and not go out after her bath in the chilly spring nights. There would be a place for her books and a writing table and a telephone, and she could see Duplessis there. Even if he had to leave her to go home, they could sit and talk like reasonable people without pinball machines crashing round her ears or lights changing or libraries closing. The winter months are not kind to a love affair, and the lighter evenings are frustrating. What starts well, in the autumn, may become less through fatigue, or the desire of one partner to be safely at home, or through sheer discomfort. All that would now be resolved. She would nurture him until summer took hold, and then, somehow, they would go away together. She would, if necessary, ask

134

George for a little money to tide her over. The audacity of her imaginings, unthinkable less than two hours ago, no longer surprised her. It would soon be her turn to be happy.

She told Duplessis the next day, smiling at him with a new confidence. She needed his approval for he had become both mother and father to her. He pushed back his hat and stirred his coffee, and at length smiled in his turn.

'Perhaps you will invite me to tea,' he said. 'Perhaps you will make me a cake. The English always do that.'

'More,' she confirmed happily.

He looked at her. He, an old married man, would soon be doing what everyone else already suspected him of doing. The obviousness of it all displeased, even disgusted him. His elegant wife would sit innocently in the rue de la Pompe, his daughters rushing in and out with unsuitable young men; he and Noémi would grimace in tired complicity over their appearance. He had been married for twenty-five years, longer than this child had been in the world. But she was not a child, he reminded himself. She was a scholar, a young woman of means, a person of some dignity and courage. He would deny her nothing. He would try to be kind. He was wise enough to know that the kindest way to treat a scholar and a person of some dignity and courage is to pretend that she is none of these things and to accord her the nurture and protection expected by less independent women. Ruth was unaware of such heroic sentiments. She was, indeed, already thinking like the ordinary woman invented by Duplessis. Plates, she thought, knives and forks; find the nearest butcher. I will learn to cook, better this time. I will leave my blue dress behind at Rhoda's or give it to Marianne.

They went out into the pale cool evening and he took her hand. She was grateful and smiled at him. Her smile moved him and strengthened his resolve. Love imposes obligations and these are constant. An intermittent lover is no use to a person of dignity and courage. He was wise enough to know this too. But he allowed her to walk home, not caring to be seen in his district with another woman in his car. She realized and respected this. She was becoming less foolish herself.

Wandering through the light spring rain, which misted and thickened her hair, she tried to work out once more whether she was committing a gross crime or merely being sensible and taking what life offered. Certainly she was far from Anthea's norm; she did not plan ahead or calculate her moves. She knew that she was capable of being alone and doing her work – that that might in fact be her true path in life, or perhaps the one for which she was best fitted – but was she not allowed to have a little more? Must she only do one thing and do it all the time? Or was the random factor, the chance disposition, so often enjoyed by Balzac, nearer to reality? She was aware that writing her dissertation on vice and virtue was an easier proposition than working it out in real life. Such matters can more easily be appraised when they are dead and gone. Dead in life and dead on the page. She had learned much from Balzac. Above all she had learned that she did not wish to live as virtuously as Henriette de Mortsauf or as Eugénie Grandet; she did not wish to be as courageous and ridiculous as Dinah de la Baudraye, who is nevertheless a great woman; she did not wish to be the Duchesse de Langeais, who has many lovers but who ends in a nunnery. She would rather be like the lady who spells death to Eugénie Grandet's hopes, a beauty glimpsed at a ball in Paris with feathers in her hair. Better a bad winner than a good loser. Balzac had taught her that too.

17

So, training herself to be a winner, she rang Jill every day
to ask how she was and bought Hugh lunch and smiled at
him constantly while trying to extract a date of departure
from him. Finally, it was settled. The last week in
March. Her room in the rue des Marronniers began to be
cluttered with little purchases: tea towels, pretty cups
and saucers, extra coat hangers. She was tired but excited; her work suffered somewhat for she could not
endure the forced immobility of the library and went out
to meet Hugh or just to walk. Sometimes Duplessis
would find her place empty at five o'clock; he would
shrug his shoulders, half disappointed, half relieved. She
was taking it all so seriously that he feared for her. No
one could measure up to her expectations; no one would
care to try. He himself would be forced to abdicate at
some point. But not yet.

On the last Saturday in March Ruth said goodbye to
Rhoda and Humphrey, who seemed sorry to see her go,
inserted herself and her belongings with some difficulty
into the van belonging to the concierge's son-in-law, and
rattled off to the rue Marboeuf. She found Hugh and Jill
having an impromptu farewell party. A glass of champagne was pressed into her hand, but she seemed to have
interrupted some private joke. Both were so helpless
with laughter that she said she would leave her things and
come back later. She made a note to buy dusters and
scouring powder; as she turned to go down the stairs

they burst out laughing again and she felt prim and rather hurt. It was the first warm day of the year. Women in this small fashionable street trod delicately, careful of their appearance. Ruth sat in a café and watched them, feeling the sun strong and bright through the plate glass of the window. She became drowsy; only expectation kept her awake for she had had little sleep the night before. She ought, she knew, to let her parents have her new address but she had so many more urgent matters to attend to, and they never wrote anyway. As the afternoon was drawing to its close she did her shopping at the grocery and climbed the stairs once more. This time expensive pigskin suitcases were standing outside the front door. When she rang the bell, Hugh answered, without his tie on. Jill was sitting on the bed fastening her dress. There was an empty champagne bottle rolling around on the floor and a great deal of scent had been upset in the tiny bathroom; the place smelt overpoweringly of lilac. They seemed unwilling to leave and proposed dinner and a later plane. Ruth sat impatiently, aware of all the tasks that awaited her before she could go to bed. But it was Sunday tomorrow, she reflected, and although she was hot and tired, the evening was lovely, with a high grey dusk and a faintly greenish cast to the skyline. The next day would be fine again. Hugh surprised her by paying the bill for dinner. He had sold a little Max Ernst drawing for cash that very morning. The omens were good.

She got to bed at two, for there was much to clear up, so much scrubbing to be done, the sheets to be changed, the bottles to be put in a bag to be taken down to the dustbin, the smell of lilac to be flapped out of the window with her duster. Even at such a late hour she could hear the traffic in the nearby Champs Elysées and imagine the moving river of brilliance. Only at dawn would the wan light illumine an empty high road which seemed to be awaiting the tramp of an exhausted returning army. She did not sleep well, tired though she was. But in the morning she eased her aching back against the pillow and realized that for the first time in her life she would shortly be drinking coffee from her own cup. No more kitchen china. No more landlords' rejects. She was a householder at last.

The next few days stayed fine and she was well content with her lot. She dusted and shopped and cooked; she walked down the Champs Elysées to the library and after the day's work she took a string bag out of her brief-case and studied the prices at the greengrocers' stalls. Duplessis smiled at her, a little sadly, for he had less of her attention these days, and said so.

'But it is all for you!' she said in astonishment. 'I am getting things ready.'

And she bought flour and sugar and a vanilla pod and many eggs. Balzac stayed in her briefcase for whole evenings at a stretch.

She could no longer identify with her favourite heroine, Eugénie Grandet. She felt she was in control of her life, that it was no longer at the mercy of others, that she could not be disposed of against her will or in ignorance of her fate. Eugénie, waiting for her handsome cousin Charles to come home to Saumur and marry her, sits dreamily in her garden, on a wormeaten bench, under a walnut tree. For relief and diversion, she looks at the miniature of her aunt, his mother, that he has given her and sees his features there. She herself, she thinks, has little to offer for she is not beautiful, although Balzac stoutly defends what looks she has and compares her kind face and large brow to those of a Madonna. But Eugénie humbly recognizes her lack of beauty as an almost fatal flaw. '*Je suis trop laide; il ne fera pas attention à moi.*' Eugénie's mother learns with dismay of her attach-ment; her nurse tries to inject some character into her; but her obdurate and miserly father is quite content to have her at home for that way he can control her fortune.

Grandet is a byword in Saumur for cunning and cheek. Eugénie is a good catch, but she is so listless, so absent, so mild. Her cousin Charles, of whom someone reports that fateful glimpse at a ball in Paris when Eugénie supposes him to be on the high seas, never returns to claim her. Eugénie, her parents dead, herself an heiress, makes a loveless match which is never consummated. She, in her turn, becomes a byword in Saumur.

Ruth, her eyes bright, her string bag filled with vegetables and fruit, felt more like Renée de l'Estorade, who is an expert on sensible arrangements. What she tended to ignore these days (and her work suffered because of it) was Balzac's strange sense of the unfinished, the sudden unforeseen deaths, the endless and unexpected remorse, the mutation of one grand lady into someone else's grander wife, the ruthless pursuit of ambition. She did not understand, and few women do, that Balzac's rascally heroes are in fact consumed with a sense of vocation, in which love only plays an evanescent if passionate part, that they will go on and on and on and never rest until death cuts them down. What she did understand, and this is not difficult, is Balzac's sense of cosmic energy, in which all the characters are submerged, until thrown up again, like atoms, to dance on the surface of one particular story, to disappear, to reappear in another guise, in another novel. No, really, Eugénie was an anomaly, so biddable, so inert on her bench in the garden, while her mother wasted away and her father grew more angry. Ruth could not remember why she had ever liked the novel in the first place.

It was arranged that Duplessis would come to the flat after his lecture at the Sorbonne, on the Thursday of a week that began fine and sunny. Tourists were already present in force in the Champs Elysées; café tables were full. Ruth, in her tartan skirt and beige pullover, felt formal and French in comparison. She would have to stay here, of that there was no doubt. She could not go home. Perhaps if she explained matters to her father he would agree to make over a little money to her. She had no thoughts beyond the completion of her dissertation, no desire for a career now, although she supposed that eventually she would teach or write or both. But she could do all that when she was thirty or so, and with much greater authority and experience. No, she would have to stay in France.

She bought a bottle of wine, and, after only one rehearsal, made for Duplessis the beautiful cake called '*la Reine de Saba*'. She sat down to wait for him. Once more, as on that other occasion, which she could now recall with a smile, a shaft of sunlight illuminated the dusty carpet. By peering upward, through the window which looked on to a well, she could see an irregular patch of Parisian grey-white sky. Resting her arms on the sill, she watched the concierge make her spidery and suspicious way into the opposite staircase, and saw the youngest girl from the architect's office next door cross the courtyard with a cone-shaped parcel of cakes on her upstretched palm. She would be able to see Duplessis as he took the same path. But perhaps he would not want to be watched. She withdrew her head and closed the window.

When she heard his steps, she smiled to herself, glad that she could not now be seen. Now her waiting was over. With a sigh, which she thought was happiness, but may in fact have been a by-product of all the waiting she had done in her life, she rose to open the door and let him in.

They ate their cake and drank their wine, not talking much, a little formal. He took her hand and kissed it, careful of her dignity. When she got up to make their coffee it was quite late and she was surprised to hear the telephone, for apart from Duplessis only Rhoda had her number.

141

'But what is it?' said Duplessis, trying to take her stricken face in his hands. She resisted him, biting her lips to regain control.

'My mother,' she said finally. 'I think she has had a heart attack.' She wept then, and gave a long sigh. 'That was my father. He said I should go home straight away.'

In fact it was Mrs Cutler, sounding frightened, who had taken the telephone away from George and whispered into it at some length.

'They had a hell of a barney,' she confided. 'I was in my room so I don't know what it was about. I heard them shouting so I got up and there was your mother, in the drawing room, for some reason, bent double in a chair. She looked awful. So did he. He looks worse than she does, if you ask me.'

'Is she dying?' asked Ruth fearfully.

Mrs Cutler released a cackle of reassuring laughter. 'Not likely,' she said, although she was not too sure herself. 'Bit of chest pain. Wind, I should say. You know how she eats.' She meant drinks. 'Doctor's been. Gave them both something to make them sleep. I'm just going to heat them some milk.' She lowered her voice. 'Try and come home soon, Ruth. It's him I'm worried about, to tell you the truth.'

'Of course, I will come straight away.'

Duplessis took her to the station. As she cleared away their coffee cups and threw away the remains of the cake, she wept again and he said nothing. He knew that she was very frightened and eventually told her that she would soon be back, that chest pains were quite common, and even a mild heart attack not fatal. And her mother was not old. Not old at all. He would see her very soon, he said encouragingly. He would telephone her at home and come to meet her train. She smiled sadly at the thought and also at the thought of the clean sheets on the bed that would not now be used. Would she ever sleep in it again?

He got her on to the Night Ferry and tipped the steward to give her a berth to herself. She struggled to raise the stiff brown blind at the window and saw him standing far below her, the brim of his hat turned up all the way round, his expression patient and contained, his hand raised. The train drew out and very soon she could no longer see him. All she could remember was a long curved platform beside a shining rail, a deserted baggage trolley, and a single figure watching the train disappear.

18

The following morning Dover looked grey, rough, and unwelcoming. Ruth, to her surprise, had slept soundly and on awakening had been haunted by a strange dream. In the dream she had been on a luxurious international train, with walnut doors and pink lamps, and was sitting down to a meal in the dining car. '*Contrefilet à la sauce ravigote*,' she ordered, then, looking sideways through the window, saw her mother, complete with denim cap, waiting patiently in some sort of siding. Helen looked thin, sardonic and helpless. Ruth struggled with the window for she wanted to get a message to her mother; she wanted to explain to her the impossibility of her leaving the train until it stopped at a proper station. But the window would not budge and Helen continued to stare, amused but implacable, through to the place where Ruth was sitting.

Ruth awoke with a start, realized where she was and why she was there, and immediately fell into a protective lethargy, her eyes dull, her limbs heavy. She ate a lot of breakfast, half fearful that the dream might come true, but a sideways glance through the window revealed only neat bungaloid hamlets, toy milk floats cruising through high streets, and acres of sodden fruit trees. As the train approached London, Ruth began to shake; the lethargy wore off, and the combined anguish of renunciation and fear of the future took her in its grip.

Yet at Oakwood Court all was surprisingly calm. Mrs

Cutler had opened the door, wearing the overall she normally only donned by request, and immediately took her cigarettes and lighter from the pocket and started smoking. She drew Ruth into the kitchen and briefed her.

'*He's* gone to Mount Street. Too ashamed to stay here, I shouldn't wonder. Seems he's got another woman and that's what the fight was about. I doubt if it was worth an argument really, but you know what she's like, anything for a bit of drama. Only this time it backfired, didn't it?'

She made them both a cup of instant coffee. Ruth, who was unused to the taste, felt a lurch of nausea which was compounded by the sight of a stained saucer serving as an ashtray on the kitchen table and the pan containing last night's milk drink lying in the sink, its thick skin regularly punctured by drips from the tap.

Mrs Cutler, glad of Ruth's company, stretched out a knobbly left hand on which was displayed a ring with a very small opaque blue stone. Ruth looked at it uncomprehendingly.

'Slow as ever, aren't you?' chided Mrs Cutler. 'My engagement ring, you funny girl. I'm getting married, aren't I? I'm going to be Mrs Dunlop.'

She made the gesture all betrothed women make, holding up her hand in front of her, trying to see the ring as a part of it that she would soon take for granted.

'That's why we had to get you home, see. Apart from the worry about *her*. I'm leaving at the end of the week. You'll be able to move into my room. Be nice and large for you. Used to be your grandma's, I understand.'

'Where is my mother?' said Ruth restlessly.

Mrs Cutler became serious.

'You'll find her in a funny mood,' she warned. 'She's got some idea that she's not going to stay here with your father. Under the same roof, she says. He had to sleep on the couch last night. Load of nonsense.' She sniffed. 'As if there was anything in it at their age. Carrying on like a

145

couple of youngsters.' Mrs Cutler had not forgotten Helen's expression of disdain when she had announced her forthcoming marriage, and, once her uneasiness had passed, could not wait to abandon Oakwood Court and head for Folkestone.

Ruth found herself pausing fearfully outside the closed door of her mother's bedroom. She knew that something monstrous waited for her on the other side. The fact of her father's absence seemed conclusive and it did not occur to her to telephone him: she felt too frightened. He had not wanted to see her, which proved that she too was at fault. She should never have gone away. And now she would see her mother, dying, in her bed.

But when she knocked and opened the door and peered in, she found Helen not in bed but seated, fully clothed, in her trouser suit and denim cap, calmly smoking and looking surprisingly well. The only odd thing about her appearance was that she was wearing shoes and was clutching a stout handbag which had once belonged to the elder Mrs Weiss and had been pronounced 'too good' to give away, although it was hopelessly old-fashioned and very heavy.

'Mother,' said Ruth, in a voice already rusty with disuse. Helen turned her head slowly and surveyed her daughter with eyes as impassive as those of an animal long in captivity. She was wearing, Ruth could see, full stage make-up and she looked ruined but beautiful. She had removed her wedding ring but had put on whatever other jewelry she possessed: the string of pearls given to her by her father on her twenty-first birthday, her mother's garnet brooch, and her silver bracelets. She had not been, in that sense, a greedy woman.

'Mother,' said Ruth again. There seemed little more to say.

At length Helen smiled, but very slightly, just like the Helen in Ruth's dream. She seemed almost amused by her daughter's predicament and refused to offer any

146

assistance whatsoever.

'Shouldn't you be in bed?' asked Ruth helplessly, although she preferred to see her mother up. 'What did the doctor say?'

Mrs Cutler now appeared in the doorway with an official-looking orange duster in her hand.

'Said she was to take it easy,' she supplied. 'And no more arguments. *He* was the one who nearly bought it, if you ask me. With his blood pressure. And the weight he's put on.'

Helen cut into this. 'Ruth,' she said, in the very deep voice Ruth had only heard her use when she was exhausted. 'We are going away. I cannot stay here.' She remembered to say cannot, Ruth noted automatically.

Ruth and Mrs Cutler both advanced on her and started talking at once. Helen again ignored them.

'I will not stay here,' she corrected, staring absently out of the window at some unhelpful daffodils blown sideways by a hefty spring breeze.

'But Mother, there is nowhere to go. You live here. You will have to come back here anyway.'

'If anyone's going it should be him,' said Mrs Cutler with relish. 'Let him go to the other one, if that's what he wants.' Helen closed her eyes. 'Then you two could stay here, all nice and cosy. And in due course get on to your solicitors. Take him for all he's worth,' she added dramatically, having heard this phrase used in a recent television film.

They both looked at her in surprise. In self-defence, Mrs Cutler studied her ring again and gave it a brief polish with her duster.

'There is to be nothing like that,' Ruth pronounced. 'You will have to discuss it like adults, without throwing fits all over the place. You can't rely on Mrs Cutler any more. And I can't always be here. I think you should be able to settle this yourselves. You aren't exactly children.'

147

'Just what I told them,' said Mrs Cutler.

Helen's eyes closed again and once more Ruth felt a fear that she might be terribly ill. After a moment Helen said, in that odd deep voice, so nearly like a man's that she gave the effect of being a ventriloquist, 'Take me away from here. I am quite ready.'

Ruth looked at Mrs Cutler. Mrs Cutler looked uneasily back.

'But where do you suppose you're going to go?' Ruth asked her mother, who was sitting quite still with her eyes closed.

'Anywhere,' said Helen. 'I will not stay here.' She was perfectly calm.

Mrs Cutler made beckoning motions to Ruth and tiptoed elaborately out of the room.

'You'd better take her away,' she whispered. 'Humour her. She's had a shock. Let her get her own back.'

'But where can I take her?' Ruth whispered back. 'I can't take her back with me to Paris.'

'What about that friend of hers in Brighton?' They were like two conspirators now, lurking in the corridor.

'Molly?' Ruth considered. 'That might be possible. But only for a couple of days at the most. I can't spend my life patching up their quarrels.'

Mrs Cutler, who had seen both Helen and George that morning, befuddled and mute and old, thought that Ruth had little chance of patching up anything. She did not, however, say so. She had pressing reasons of her own for getting Helen away until she could make good her own escape. George, she could ignore. She doubted if he'd be back, in any case.

'Mother,' said Ruth, with tremendous cheerfulness and in the loud voice certain people use with the deranged or disabled. 'Do you feel well enough to go to Molly's? What about a couple of days in Brighton, until this nonsense blows over?'

Helen turned her head very slowly until she faced her

148

daughter. Her eyes, skilfully ringed with blue shadow, gleamed with dull amusement. She had remembered to blend the dark pink make-up into her temples and her throat. She looked aquiline but unsuitable, with an expression like a lizard. Ruth had never seen her so still. Her loose clothes hid her extreme thinness.

'Well enough? That is neither here nor there. You may remember I appeared in *Ring Round the Moon* with a broken ankle.'

So Ruth rang up Molly who, to her eternal credit and to the credit of the teachings of Mary Baker Eddy, laughed gaily, and said, what a fuss, but come by all means. She would expect them around tea-time.

'Sooner,' said Helen, in her strange deep voice.

'Sooner,' echoed Ruth helplessly.

'As soon as you like,' said Molly, and replaced the receiver with fingers that were now shiny and swollen with arthritis.

19

Mrs Jacobs took one look at George's odd patchy pallor and telephoned Roddy, who was supposed to be having his day off, to come in and look after the shop. She was taking George to Bayswater. Apart from her worry about his condition, she could not run the risk of being telephoned by Helen, and she doubted that Helen would find her in the directory under her late husband's name, although she was uneasily aware that George might have discussed her with his wife in the days when she was a stranger trying to buy the business. Well, she could not think of everything.

Roddy grumbled – the boy was really becoming impossible – but turned up half an hour later in his slightly shiny dark blue suit, his blue shirt and stiff white collar, his abundant fair hair brushed down with water, a small razor cut marring the pink smoothness of his plump face. He was heartily fed up with his aunt's changes of mind, with what he considered to be her senile passion, and above all with George, who called him 'old fellow' and preached the virtues of staying in the book trade while demonstrating what little virtue it still held for him. Like most young people, Roddy hated hypocrites, and did not allow for the fact that he was growing into one himself.

It was therefore with no sense of the incongruous that he ushered his aunt off the premises, patted her arm (for he had his expectations to consider) and even stuck his head in through the window of the car to wish them well.

As if we were going on holiday, thought Mrs Jacobs, rather resentfully. George drove off. Roddy mentally washed his hands of the pair of them, went back into the shop, rang up his girl friend to come over and keep him company, and then settled down to the *New Statesman*.

George was silent, concentrating on the driving. He felt very hot and his eyes were not too good; sometimes he saw a double image of the Bayswater Road. He had little idea of what he was going to do, but he had no intention of going home until Ruth had arrived. He would perhaps have a talk with her, explain that he was going away for a while, and return to the Bayswater flat to be cared for by Mrs Jacobs. The sad thing was that he did not know how much blame to take for last night's débâcle. He had not been terribly unfaithful to Helen. He did not intend to leave her for good. He just wished he could get rid of the sight of Helen in his mind's eye, bent double and moaning in an unaccustomed chair while the silent but not inactive television screen flickered with a programme which he might otherwise have found quite interesting.

'She brought it on herself,' said Mrs Jacobs, as if divining his thoughts. 'She was no wife to you.'

George agreed, nodding his head, but found that this action disturbed his vision even more. He longed for Sally's flat, where nothing bad could happen. And even if it did, she would take care of it. Maybe he could get her to ring Oakwood Court later and speak to Ruth. Maybe he need not go home at all, until everything had blown over. Maybe not even then. With these thoughts in mind he abandoned the situation. Sally was quite right: he had done enough.

'After all I've done for her,' he began to murmur. 'Bringing her meals in bed. Doing all the housekeeping. Is that a life for a man?'

Mrs Jacobs felt the beneficial shift from sadness to anger and egged him on.

'There was no need for you to have done any of it,' she said. 'You're her husband, not a lady-in-waiting.'

'All that stuff from Fortnum and Mason's,' George continued, as they went up in the lift. 'And she never even bothered to get out of bed. I even took her away on holiday. Apparently that was wrong too.'

Mrs Jacobs put her key in the lock.

'I've never said anything, as you know,' she began, as a prelude to saying it all now, 'but you've been a fool. Some women take advantage. Once they're married and they've got a good husband, they think they can do what they like. And if they take him for granted,' she paused significantly, 'they just don't bother any more.'

George moved into the warm sitting room, his head aching. He wanted to tell Sally that it had not always been like that. That he and Helen had been married for a long time, that they had a child, that that made a difference. But how do you say this to a childless woman without hurting her? He also wanted to say that Helen was brave and honest, or had been. Maybe she still was. He wanted to tell her that he had been reminded, by Helen's reeling last night, as from a blow to the heart, while the television mumbled on unheeded, that he thought his wife still loved him. He wanted to say it but he knew that he could not.

Sally was in the kitchen, filling the kettle. Sally felt that most crises could be palliated by the administration of food or drink. But after that he must make up his mind to go home. She could not compromise herself by having him permanently in the flat. Supposing she were cited in a divorce case? Her sister would never forgive her. No, it would not do. She had herself to think of. And anyway, it was the daughter's responsibility. She would have a word with her later.

George sank heavily into a chair and thought about Helen. Sally he could now barely remember. He thought of Helen as he had first known her, how he had waited for her shamelessly at the stage door. He thought of their courtship and their many honeymoons, for they liked to think of themselves as perpetual lovers. He remembered how they had groaned when they had discovered that Helen was pregnant, and of all the fuss she had made, wanting to get rid of the baby. He remembered his mother's stern face when she overhead some of this exchange. She had entered Helen's bedroom, minatory in her black dress with the small white dots and the dull cut steel brooch at the collar, and had extracted from her a promise that she would behave herself like a responsible married woman. They had been as ashamed as a couple of children, and Helen had had her baby. A funny little thing, with Helen's red hair, but none of her looks. Mrs Weiss eventually took over the functions of a nurse. George could remember the large slow woman with the little child huddled on her lap: Mrs Weiss was telling her a story, very quietly, because she was ashamed of her strong accent. George and Helen had been left remark-ably free. George thought again of his mother, and of all those meals she had invented for him. He saw himself sitting at the dining room table, while she buttered a poppy seed roll for him, before he went away to school, to university, to work. He remembered her hands, swol-len and shiny from immersion in too many bowls of cold water; he remembered her impassive face red with the steam escaping from saucepans as she lifted the lids. At home she had had servants, but he had never heard her complain. He remembered her at his bedside when he was ill, sitting sometimes all through the night.

George slept. When Mrs Jacobs came in with the tray and a prepared speech, she was unable to rouse him. She sat down and drank her coffee quietly, trying not to feel uneasy. It was when he began a harsh steady snoring that she panicked and shook him. He did not respond. Then she shrieked and rang for an ambulance and rang for Roddy who, to his eternal credit, was there before the ambulance and went with them to the hospital.

'A mild stroke,' said the doctor, half an hour later. 'He'll be home in a few days. We get them moving very quickly. Are you his wife and son?'

Mrs Jacobs said no, they were only acquaintances really. He lived with his family at Oakwood Court. Yes, it would really be better if the hospital took charge now and let the family know; she and her nephew had no wish to get involved. They had had a shock as it was, and with her anxiety state she tended to take things rather hard.

The doctor patted her arm. 'You did splendidly,' he said, 'I wish there were more people like you about.' Then he shook Roddy's hand and vanished down the corridor, his white coat flapping. Roddy and Mrs Jacobs looked at each other, partners in crime. At least, that was how it felt.

20

The winter had not been kind to Molly Edwards. On the south coast the winds had blown keenly and when they died down a mist rolled in from the sea and made her long to have the winds back again. She ached now and had been forced to go to the doctor, although of course she did not believe in them.

'You have arthritis,' he said bluntly. 'I can give you some pills to help with the pain.'

Molly drew the line at that and said so. She had left her principles far enough behind as it was.

'In that case,' said the doctor, 'I can only advise you to move away from here and go somewhere warmer and more sheltered.'

Molly had shut up her beach chalet and removed the electric kettle. It was not only her shoulder now, it was her knee and her fingers that pained her. She thought she might wait to see if the summer brought an improvement and if not, well, she need not live through another winter. No one would miss her. She did not even have a cat.

It was a long winter, sitting in her flat, which she had never liked. She found it difficult to do a lot for herself but her lodger was very kind and brought back her shopping from the health food store every Saturday morning. He was a student at Brighton Polytechnic and would be leaving in the summer, so there was no need to worry about him. But the days were endless and she felt anxious until he returned in the evenings and sometimes she waited for him late into the night. She sat in her drawing room, in her dull beige chair, trying to read. But her attention wandered – the wind made such a noise – and she gave up. She was not a hysterical woman and she did not dwell on the past. But when she saw the stunted hedge outside her window quivering under the impact of the sea wind she thought of other, kindlier places that she had known. And of her husband, a little. No children. That had been her eternal regret but no one had ever known. She had kept so cheerful that she took them all in. Even now, when she ordered her supplies that the student would later carry home for her, the people at the health food store assured her that she was marvellous, that she cheered them all up. She walked with a stick these days and as she manoeuvred her way out of the shop, she did not see them shaking their heads behind her back.

It was teeming with a persistent rain on the morning that Ruth rang up and Molly had been feeling so unwell that she was relieved and delighted by the diversion. She was sorry to hear of Helen's illness, but Helen, she knew, was a tough girl, and she did not take it too seriously. And little Ruth had always been so sensible. She had not seen her for years, although the child always had nice things to say when they talked on the telephone. None of her mother's spirit, of course. More like her grandmother, a very conventional woman.

She was grunting slightly with pain as she got the dining room table shut and shoved it again the wall. It took her the rest of the morning to shift the chairs back with her good knee. Then she had a rest and spoke to herself sternly, reminding herself that pain does not exist. After this she was able to push the divans into the centre of the room. She did not bother with a bedside table. The lamp with the parchment shade and the trailing flex was not too much trouble but she knew she could not make up the beds. She would have to ask Ruth, although it did seem such a shame, when she had had no guests for ages. She would have liked to put flowers in the room but she simply could not move. And there was precious little food. Perhaps Ruth would be able to go to the shops when she had installed her mother. In the meantime Molly could give an uninterrupted ear to everything Helen had to tell her and she did not doubt that there was a story behind her visit. Most of Helen's little illnesses in the past had had an ulterior motive. And she usually got her way in the end. Molly smiled reminiscently, It would be like old times, pulling Helen together again, talking to her like an older sister. She hobbled out and put the front door on the latch, in case her hands seized up later and she could not let them in. Then she sat down in her chair by the window and waited for them to come to her.

Helen's face, rosy, thin, and stern; her strange deep voice; her restless hands gripping the unfashionable black leather bag; her improbable denim cap. These images haunted Ruth as she spread the thin worn sheets over the narrow divans, and put a new bulb in the lamp, and later went out into the relentless rain to buy, with what little English money she had left, something to make into a sandwich for Helen and Molly. She herself would be unable to eat. The journey had not been too bad. Helen had been very quiet and had not even smoked much. She had not read or talked. Ruth was a little hurt that her mother should ignore her to such an extent but she was too relieved to find Helen alive – and in a strange way in command – to experience real cause for complaint. But she felt benighted with travelling and untidiness. A moral disorder seemed to have overtaken them and was immediately translated into physical distress. Ruth had put their nightclothes into a suitcase, without care, jumbling up her own spotless cotton with her mother's

157

dingy silk. She tried to shield her mother on the journey, taking her by the arm, protecting her from the rain. It could not be done. Rain dripped from her hair, which had lost its shape; the hem of her coat was sodden. And they had brought no other clothes with them. Perhaps, she thought, I will telephone Mrs Cutler this evening and find out what is happening. Basically she did not care to know what was happening but it seemed to be her job to find out. She sighed a shuddering sigh, turned into Molly's street, and unlocked the door with the unfamiliar key.

As she unpacked the quarter pound of ham and the butter and the tomatoes and the small white loaf, she could hear her mother's strange new voice from the drawing room. Helen did not seem to be set on any particular narrative, but erupted in odd craggy irrelevancies, which were smoothed over by the more comforting burden of Molly's reassurance. Molly soothed, but could not reach Helen. Molly, far from enjoying Helen's company, was oddly alarmed by her behaviour. Helen sat as if visiting briefly, her cap in place, her bag still clutched in her hands. Like a refugee, thought Molly. Helen had not even wanted to rest on her bed, although from what Molly had understood she had been bedridden until she came away. She did not smoke, she did not demand a drink, although she had a cup of tea, which Molly made with the electric kettle from the chalet, now plugged into the socket of the lamp behind her chair. From time to time Helen uttered a short sardonic laugh, though Molly could not really say what was amusing her. She was relieved when she heard the door close behind Ruth and went painfully into the kitchen to talk to her. It took her nearly a minute to get out of her chair and take a few deep breaths, for the effort of moving the furniture was beginning to have its effect.

Ruth, who was by now grey with misery, explained that her parents had had some sort of argument, that her father had not even stayed at home to meet her, and her mother refused to sleep under the same roof. Molly gave a comforting laugh. 'I've heard that one before,' she said. 'When they were first married I heard it quite a lot. Helen was always a spirited girl, and George sometimes put his foot in it. Don't worry, Ruth; it will all blow over.'

Ruth sighed. 'They're not newly married now. I can't nurse them through this. It's about time they behaved like adults.' Ruth still believed that adults adhered to a superior standard of behaviour.

Molly, who was in some pain, suggested that they all have an early night, and discuss it again in the morning. Ruth agreed. They ate their sandwiches in relative silence. Ruth unpacked their suitcase and turned down her mother's bed. Helen seemed to have no strength or will left; she sat down abruptly on the edge of her divan and said, 'You will have to undress me, I'm afraid.' She held out her arms, like a child. Molly, hovering in the doorway, encouraged Ruth with nods, although her expression was thoughtful. She herself would have liked a little help with her stockings but was too shy to ask.

With horror Ruth took off her mother's clothes, which were barely warm and smelled of old scent. She tried not to look at the shrunken breasts, the bony elbows and knees, the slumped and shameful pelvis. She removed the denim cap and slipped over Helen's head a nightdress of crêpe de chine trimmed with lace in a colour Helen had always called orchid pink: 'my colour'. She brushed her mother's long hair and tied it back with a piece of tape. Helen put up a slow hand and removed the tape. 'I always wear my hair loose at night,' she said.

When the telephone rang, Ruth darted out of the room, glad to be delivered from the spectacle she had just witnessed. She felt a sudden wave of fury, which she directed against all painters of martyrdoms and depositions. 'About suffering, they were never wrong, the Old Masters,' said Auden. But they were. Frequently. Death was usually heroic, old age serene and wise. And of course, the element of time, that was what was missing. Duration. How many more nights would she have to undress her mother, only to dress her again in the morning? Would she soon have to wash her, to bath her, to feed her? Was there any way in which this could be avoided?

Apparently there was not. For Mrs Cutler, at the other end of the telephone, announced that George was in hospital for a few days, but that it was not serious. 'A bit of a turn,' said Mrs Cutler, quite accurately. As she herself was leaving at the end of the following week, she thought it might be better if Ruth and her mother came home. George would no doubt need a bit of looking after once he came out of hospital. And she didn't like to leave without saying goodbye to them. After all this time.

She told Helen the news, making it sound less important than it really was, but Helen lost her composure and screamed and wept, and Ruth had to sit up most of the night with her arms around her mother. When she eventually climbed into her own bed, she could not sleep, for Helen, although sedated with the sleeping pills Ruth had found in her bag, was still agitated, and moaned and muttered, streaking her rosy make-up as she moved her face compulsively on the pillow. 'Is it time?' sighed Helen and, much later, 'Darling heart.' Lying so close to her mother, hearing the words of love, and knowing, in the course of that long night, that she would hear no others, Ruth covered her face and wept.

In the morning it was still teeming with rain. Ruth got up and made tea, for Molly, who smiled at her lovingly, and for Helen, who looked blankly ahead. Helen was shaky now and Ruth had to steady the cup in her hand.

'We had better make a start,' she said. 'When you're ready, go and use the bathroom.'

But an hour later, washed and dressed herself, she had to rouse her mother out of a daydream and repeat her recommendations.

This morning Helen moved stiffly, like an old woman. When she emerged from the bathroom, Ruth saw that she had not washed her face which was now less rosy, less aquiline, and more than a little blurred. Again Ruth brushed her mother's hair and helped her into her clothes. Helen said nothing. She pointed to Mrs Weiss's heavy bag which Ruth handed to her. Helen opened it, pulled out her make-up box, which was sizable, and proceeded to ring her eyes with blue and restore her mouth. She blended rouge into her forehead, cheeks and chin, put on her denim cap, and looked at Ruth as if to say, 'I am ready.'

Ruth packed the case, stripped the beds, restored the furniture to its rightful place, Molly thanking her repeatedly all the while. Ruth went to the shops and got Molly some more tea, and Molly in her turn insisted on presenting Ruth with at least two pounds of wizened apples. 'They are unsprayed,' she announced proudly. Ruth did not know what she meant, but did not intend to ask. 'Perhaps,' she suggested, 'you could let me have a carrier bag?' After what seemed a lengthy interval Molly was back with a plastic bag imprinted with a cornucopia and the legend, 'Here's Health!'; she handed it to Ruth, trying to hide her monstrous knuckles.

Molly was not sorry they were leaving. She had not slept well and she had not liked the sounds that Helen was making in her sleep. She felt too ill herself to be of much use, and Helen was as uncompromising as ever, although Ruth was a dear, a real dear. Molly would have liked to ask Ruth to stay on but obviously the girl was going to have to look after her father until she got another house-keeper. Helen, of course, would be quite useless. And it was Saturday, and they would be expecting her down at the health food shop. She was quite anxious for them to

161

leave, really. Strange, when she was so lonely most of the time.

She kissed Helen, who gave a sigh and kissed her back. She kissed Ruth, who tried not to pull her face away. But she was too slow in getting back to the drawing room to see them drive off in the taxi, and to wave goodbye.

The journey, again, was not too bad. They had a carriage to themselves, and Ruth had bought her mother a magazine. Helen glanced at the cover, then looked out of the streaming window; raindrops trembled and quivered in long diagonal streaks, and she could not see what lay beyond.

At Victoria, things began to go wrong. Rain drummed on the glass roofs over the platforms, spurted up from the rails. They had to join a queue for taxis, Ruth struggling with the suitcase, the umbrella, the carrier bag, and her mother. Helen shivered. Ruth tried to shield her from the weather. She looked about her beseechingly but met only indifferent or incurious eyes. She realized with alarm that she had very little money left and wondered if she dare change some travellers' cheques. But she was uneasy about her mother and did not like to leave her alone. The people in the queue seemed ill-disposed; there was no one she would have cared to trust. They shuffled forward, manoeuvring their luggage in front of them. Taxis were infrequent and small arguments broke out. When the taxis arrived they did not always want to go where the passengers wanted them to, and some even drove off empty.

Ruth put the carrier bag down and took her mother in her arms, fearing for her in this damp and cold and acrimonious place. Helen rested lightly against her daughter, her head almost empty of thought. She had never been a maternal woman, had never felt that hunger that makes a woman reach to caress and stroke a child's flesh and which is never assuaged. Helen had been too

162

beautiful, too happy, too successful, ever to feel pre-monitory loss. Now all she knew was that she was cold and uncomfortable, that she was light-headed from the train and the unaccustomed noise, and that she could not quite concentrate on where she was or why she was there. Or why George was not there. Ruth, glancing at her mother, saw her bewilderment; she felt her mother's heart thudding irregularly through her thin sleeve, and she tightened her arms, trying to give comfort.

Now Helen drifted, remembering her younger days and triumphs, when there were always people there to take care of things. 'Your sheltered life,' George used to say to her jokingly, when she demanded to have a dress chosen or asked him to brush her hair. She had never really got used to doing things for herself, only became vibrant and independent when on stage. When taking a curtain call she looked and felt indomitable. She was childishly inept in the house. She had never learned to cook and of course would not shop and clean. When she reflected on this, and on the way George had judged her and found her wanting, the pain in her heart, which was now beating like a drum, became sharper. It had all got out of control, like her retirement, which had been in-voluntary, and her loss of weight and vigour, both of which she now experienced as extreme weakness. A brief spurt of anger ('Why me? I always gave good value') dissolved into a weariness which she could no longer measure. She sagged against Ruth, her mouth dry, her throat aching. The denim cap fell off, dropped, got muddy. 'Leave it,' she said, 'it doesn't matter any more.' Then she was silent, half supported, sinking towards sleep.

The taxi which arrived after three-quarters of an hour was driven by a man with severe back pain and a delin-quent son. Both were preying on his mind. He brooded as Ruth opened the door, pushed in the suitcase, the carrier bag, the umbrella, and finally Helen.

'Oakwood Court?' he said. 'That's Kensington way, isn't it? Sorry, love, can't do it. I'm going back to the garage. Clapham.'

Helen gave a moan and raised her fingers to her mouth. Ruth looked at her and panicked.

'I think my mother is ill,' she said, kneeling on the floor with her mouth to the taxi-driver's window, as if in a confessional. 'Please, do be kind and take us home. We have no other way of getting there and I can't put her back in the queue.'

He looked round. 'No thanks,' he said swiftly, for he did not like sick passengers and had enough troubles of his own. 'Can't be done,' he added.

Ruth had one pound in her purse. 'I will give you double the money,' she urged, although she had no hope of even paying the full fare. The magazine slid off Helen's lap and Helen made no effort to retain it. Ruth looked round at her mother. Helen's eyes were closed, her hand spread on her chest.

Ruth screamed. 'Take me home. Take me home. Take me home.' Tears spurted from her eyes and her mouth opened like a child's. 'Take me home,' she chanted. 'Take me home.'

People looked curiously in at the windows of the cab. A policeman approached from the back of the queue. Cursing, the driver fumbled with the gears and the cab moved off. Ruth continued to sob and for a long time stayed kneeling on the floor, with her head against the glass. She did not dare look back. She knew what she would find.

By the time they reached Oakwood Court, Helen had died.

21

When George came out of hospital, he was very quiet and very slow, although the doctor had assured him that he could and should lead a normal life. It was difficult to assess how the news of Helen's death had affected him. When Ruth broke it to him he was lying in a small cheerful ward, in strange striped pyjamas; Mrs Jacobs, with Roddy as chaperone, was unpacking small quantities of food and placing them in his locker, against all the regulations. The little parcels and dishes would be removed later by the nurses, but George had given up trying to tell her. In any case, he was afraid she would stop cooking for him.

When he heard of Helen's death, he had pursed his lips in the old absent fashion which used to denote deep thought. Then he had sighed and reached for Sally's hand, and clutching it, had slept for a bit. One tear slid down his cheek. They stood rigidly round his bed, as if he were going to die. A nurse came round with the tea trolley and woke him up and then they knew he was all right.

On the way out Mrs Jacobs laid a tremulous and restraining hand on Ruth's arm. 'You won't leave him now, will you, dear? You won't go back to Paris?' Ruth, who found the other woman's concern and anxiety rather affecting, said nothing. She had hoped to be able to return to Paris within the month, having found George a suitable housekeeper or else leaving the matter in Mrs

Jacobs's hands. But it seemed that this was not to be. Yet she would have to go back, if only to collect her notes on Balzac. The rest of her things – her cups and saucers, towels, knives and forks – she would have to leave behind.

She explained this to Mrs Jacobs, whose eyes widened with alarm. 'Go now,' urged Mrs Jacobs, 'while he's still in hospital. But come back soon. He's going to feel very lonely.' So she went to Paris for inside a day, collected her notes, tried to ring Duplessis at the Sorbonne, failed to reach him, had to leave, and came back on the Night Ferry, with her briefcase in her hand. She arrived back in London just in time to collect George, who was being discharged from hospital on that day. Roddy, very handsomely, offered to drive him back to Oakwood Court. Mrs Jacobs hovered in attendance.

When Ruth opened the door of the flat the air struck her as particularly musty. Mrs Cutler had gone, rather earlier than expected, without washing up the milk saucepan or removing the stained saucer from the kitchen table. There was a note by the telephone: 'All the best! Keep your chin up!' Mrs Jacobs, her nose wrinkling with distaste, opened the door of the refrigerator which had not been defrosted for some weeks and cleared out the shiny cheese and the wilting lettuce on which Ruth had been living. George moved slowly into Helen's bedroom, took off his jacket and left it on the bed, and got into his dressing gown. Then he went into the drawing room and sat down in front of the television and was soon fast asleep.

Mrs Jacobs did not like what she saw: neglect, decay, staleness. Nobody had cleaned this place out for weeks, even months. She opened as many windows as she dared, not caring to go into the bedrooms, and shook her head slowly when she saw the state of the dining room, the handsome table scarred with rings from hot dishes, and now piled high with Ruth's books. She could get no sense out of George, whose pills made him drowsy, and Ruth seemed oddly absent, as if she did not care to dwell on their present predicament. She had not even put an advertisement for a new housekeeper in the *Lady*. And, for once, Mrs Jacobs did not dare to offer to do it for her.

A routine was slowly established. Ruth would get up and dust the flat and make her father's breakfast and serve it to him in bed. She found it difficult to break into his inertia, which she attributed to the shock of his wife's death, and after a time she came to accept it. She would tidy his bedroom while he had his bath, wait until he got dressed, although he would not put on a tie or a jacket, and, sitting him down in the drawing room with the newspaper, she would go out and do the shopping. After lunch George would rest and Ruth could get on with her work. In the late afternoon Mrs Jacobs, escorted by Roddy, would call round with a casserole wrapped in a snowy napkin or a plate of apple cake, which they would eat in the evening. George lived for her visits, and tried to hold her hand, thus putting her into a state of acute embarrassment. With her hand imprisoned, her eyes would wander uneasily to the faded wallpaper, the frayed carpet, the uncleaned windows. Roddy and Ruth would watch impassively, each disapproving of the other. Ruth was thinner and her hair had grown long. She did not pay much attention to what she wore these days. Roddy, on the other hand, was putting on weight; his new pin-striped suit was already a little too tight for him. He had more or less taken over the shop, for his aunt pronounced that her nerves were too bad to allow her to cope. He resented the time he spent ferrying her back and forth to Oakwood Court and wished that George would shove off so that he could be rid of the lot of them. He disliked Ruth but was hurt that she didn't appear to be more friendly. It was, he thought, the least she could do.

After Mrs Jacobs and Roddy had left – earlier every

167

day, Ruth noted – George extolled Sally's virtues. Such a cook, he enthused, such a home-maker. And how Roddy had improved! He really had a future. 'A very nice nature,' said George in his new reedy voice. 'You might do worse, Ruth . . .' His voice trailed away as he saw in Ruth's eye the sardonic gleam he had often noticed in Helen's. In any case, he did not wish to consider the future. As long as Ruth was there and Sally came every day he had no worries.

But one day Mrs Jacobs took Ruth on one side and explained to her, a little tearfully, that she was going to stay with her sister Phyllis in Manchester because her depression was so bad that she did not care to be alone. She promised to telephone when she got back to London although she could not say when that would be. She knew that Ruth would understand. 'I've made him a meat loaf,' she said, her voice shaking, 'and an almond pudding. Warm the pudding up a little in the oven, dear, but don't give him too much. He's putting on weight again and it's so bad for him.'

'But what about your flat?' asked Ruth, who fully expected to have to act as a caretaker. Mrs Jacobs said that Roddy would be staying there while she was away. At that moment Roddy loomed in the doorway with a large carton in his arms. He was well pleased with things as they stood. He had urged his mother in Manchester to get his aunt away from London and he had every hope of taking over the business completely, for he knew his aunt would not come back. He was delighted to exchange his almost but not quite chic basement in Notting Hill for the greater comforts of the Bayswater flat, which he planned to improve considerably. And although he had promised his aunt that he would keep in touch with George and Ruth, he had no intention of doing so. They had his telephone number if they wanted him.

He placed the carton, which contained George's sun lamp and his portable grill, on the kitchen table, and prepared to be very nice to them all for the last time. Mrs Jacobs wept openly when she saw George's things, like abandoned toys, in this untidy place. It was Roddy who had urged her to get rid of them. He was quite keen on the record player and said she could keep that. She did not like to argue with him: he had been so good. But she hid George's favourite record of Viennese waltzes in a drawer in her bedroom so that Roddy could not give it away. She knew him well enough. As the car left Oakwood Court far behind she sighed and was silent. Roddy, stealing a glance at her, thought she looked much older. He would not be sorry to put her on the train. After that, his mother would have to cope.

George remained mercifully unaware of his infirmities. 'Is Sally back yet?' he would ask, and Ruth would say, 'Not yet.' 'Can't be long now,' he would assure her, as if she needed the assurance. He would wander back to the drawing room and the television set and wait for the next meal. Nobody visited now. Nobody telephoned. It would not do much good if they did. Once the telephone had rung and a voice had said, 'Alain Duplessis.' This was repeated several times, but George, who had been trained to put the receiver to his good ear, knew no one of that name and so assumed it was a wrong number and thought no more about it.

There was no question of Ruth's going back to France. After a while she got in touch with Anthea and Anthea came swooping into Oakwood Court, cheeks aflame, to tell Ruth what to do. Or rather what not to do. George was delighted to see her. 'Ruth's pretty friend,' he murmured, and tried to take her hand. Anthea was marvellous with him, and cheered him up, and teased him, and gave every appearance of enjoying it as much as he did. George was almost normal by the time she left.

In the hall Anthea hissed, 'For God's sake, get out

before he's bedridden. Find a housekeeper. Do *something*. Have you any idea what you look like? What about the flat in Paris? Is it still there? Have you got a lease?'

Ruth thought of her flat and the sunlight and the cake she had made. The clean sheets were still on the bed. She hoped that the food she had left in the larder was not attracting mice.

'I can't go back,' she replied. 'I've got to stay here. I can't leave him. Besides, I've got a job. Professor Wyatt has offered me an assistant lectureship. I'm very lucky really.'

They looked at each other. Anthea's eyes filled with tears.

'You shouldn't be alone,' she murmured. 'Is there no one?'

Ruth laughed. 'Only Roddy,' she said.

They kissed. Anthea tried to comfort Ruth but Ruth was bony and unyielding and in the end Anthea rested her head on Ruth's shoulder and had a good cry, and then wiped her eyes, and put on some more lipstick, and left, and went back to Weybridge, and Brian, and her twin sons, Christopher and Martin.

In the country of the old and sick there are environmental hazards. Cautious days. Early nights. A silent, ageing life in which the anxiety of the invalid overrides the vitality of the untouched. A wariness, in case the untoward might go undetected. Sudden gratitude that turns bitterness into self-reproach. George fretted more over Ruth now than he had ever done during her childhood. If she went out, she would look back and see him at the window, watching her. When she returned, he would still be there. He had time to think of the meals that might tempt him but no appetite to eat much of them. He resisted attempts to get him out of his dressing gown. He refused to walk far. Above all, he required constant reassurance that she would not leave him.

170

After a couple of years it became clear that he would make no further progress, nor any less. Ruth, after a telephone call from Anthea, now pregnant with her third child, went back to the house in Edith Grove and found Miss Howe, much diminished, still in her basement. Miss Mackendrick has been dead for three months and her rooms, cluttered and musty, had not been cleared out or re-let. Ruth contacted her former landlord and took Miss Mackendrick's rooms on a temporary basis. Her old flat was occupied by a young couple who played the guitar and made rather a lot of noise, yelling to each other on the stairs. Ruth spent one evening, at the most two, a week in Edith Grove. Sometimes, on these evenings, she would baby-sit for Hugh and Jill in Beaufort Street. But most of the time she wrote her book. When she went back to Oakwood Court, George would be at the window, in his dressing gown, waiting for her.

22

She married Roddy almost as a matter of course, since George was so attached to the idea. She married him without a great deal of emotion, but in recognition of the fact that he had paid her the compliment of asking her to be his wife; what his motives were she could never understand. In fact Roddy was lonely, and, hypochondriacal like his aunt, was given to scares about his health and his future. Ruth's calm, her unostentatious energy, seemed like strength. Once she nursed him through a bad bout of 'flu, adding a daily visit to Bayswater to her long list of chores. He was impressed. When he recovered, he rang her up and suggested that they might go to a concert. He fell into the habit of collecting her from the college when he had finished work and driving her home. Sometimes he stayed for a meal, for she had become a very good cook. He felt comfortable in her presence, at ease, relaxed. Eventually he asked her to marry him. In this he showed sense; it is best to marry for purely selfish reasons.

During the six months of their marriage Ruth felt a great sense of security, which, she was assured by Anthea, is what every woman needs. Her colleagues, she was amused to note, were rather more polite to her than they had been when she was merely a daughter. It seemed easier to live at Oakwood Court from every point of view. Although Mrs Jacobs would not have objected to their permanent occupation of the Bayswater flat, there was an air of uncertainty over her own arrangements. She was always rumoured to be coming back to London, but she never actually came, and one day her sister Phyllis, a managerial woman, took matters in hand and disposed of the flat and its contents in the space of a fortnight. Roddy did not much mind; he had found it hard to keep everything laundered and all the machinery maintained and sometimes he had yearning thoughts about his basement. But he was no good at looking after himself, and he thought that once they had found George a housekeeper he and Ruth could settle down quite comfortably somewhere on their own.

At Oakwood Court things were a little brighter. The mere presence of Roddy cheered George tremendously, and although Roddy still found him tiresome he was quite amicable about watching television with George and brought him home the evening paper and sometimes drove him out in the car at weekends. Ruth was relieved to see them taking care of each other, for George was as anxious about Roddy's health as Roddy was himself. Roddy felt protected. Ruth, her mind sifting through the day's preoccupations, thought that she had been lucky. Roddy, she knew, was an amiable but childish character, but she clung to him in the night when she wakened so inexplicably in terror, with fragments of dream evaporating into the greater unreality of her present life. At these times, she thought in all humility that she was a fortunate woman.

Roddy died, not of an illness as he had feared, but as a result of a motor accident on the Kingston by-pass: they never found out what he was doing there. A policeman brought the news to Oakwood Court. Ruth and George were both quite dazed, and for once in their lives talked openly to each other, turning to each other for a little comfort. They could not believe that such a thing had happened, that they were both, once again, survivors. They wondered how they had been singled out for such a privilege.

In due course Ruth sold the shop, since there was no prospect of George's taking it over again. The money was very useful and they paid a woman to come in every day and do the cleaning. George got quite attached to her and was rather surprised when she would not consent to live in. Ruth went back to spending two nights a week at Edith Grove. She had kept the rooms on, for, as she explained to Roddy, most of her books were there. Her work on Balzac, after hanging fire for a year or two, eventually picked up again and she was able to plan the second volume.

One Saturday, as Ruth was preparing a *daube* of beef, there was a ring at the doorbell. George shuffled out of the drawing room and stood expectantly in the hall. Their visitor, to their very great surprise, was Mrs Cutler, in a fun fur coat and high-heeled boots, with several carrier bags on the mat at her feet.

'Long time no see,' she said exuberantly, as Ruth murmured a welcome. George, disappointed that it was not Sally, returned to the drawing room. Mrs Cutler followed him.

'Well, that's a nice welcome, I must say,' she bellowed, for she remembered him as being on the deaf side and the poor sod looked years older. 'After all this time.'

'Have you come back?' asked George.

Mrs Cutler uttered a screech of laughter which ended in a cough. 'Not bloody likely,' she said, opening a large handbag and extracting a packet of Senior Service. 'Leslie won't let me do a thing in me own place, let alone anybody's else's. No,' she added, inhaling deeply. 'I came up for the sales and I thought I'd look in on you and see if there was a cup of tea going. And I wouldn't mind spending a penny,' she conceded. She looked at them as if expecting sounds of appreciation.

After she had returned from the bathroom, leaving the

door open as usual, and after she had drunk a cup of tea and smoked three cigarettes, she regaled them with stories of life at the Clarence Nursing Home. 'Of course,' she said, screwing up her eyes against the smoke, 'we've made a lot of improvements there. Colour telly. Fluorescent lighting in all the bedrooms. The old dears think the world of us.' Ruth looked at her in her checked mini-skirt, her unventilated royal blue angora jersey, her necklace of vaguely ethnic ceramic platelets. She could not do it. The temptation to put George into a nursing home had never been very strong, although Anthea had introduced her to the idea long ago. But George, thought Ruth, had had style; he could not end up like that. She knew what the Clarence would be like: the television on all day, the residents encouraged to sit outside in the brisk sea wind, the food consisting of mince and mashed potatoes and masses and masses of prunes. And Mrs Cutler or Mrs Dunlop or whatever she was passing among them graciously with a kind word ('Never say die!') and a cigarette somewhere about her person.

George sensed what Ruth was thinking but was too frightened to trust her judgment. His face became flushed and distressed and Ruth put a hand on his arm. Mrs Cutler, who knew danger signs when she saw them, hobbled to her feet, collected her carrier bags, and took her leave. At the door, she whispered to Ruth, 'You've been a good girl,' and added, 'but if I were you . . . Well, if you ever want a break,' she winked and nudged Ruth in the ribs, 'you know where I am. Keep in touch, anyway. I enjoy a laugh over the old times.' Then she was gone, nippily, down the stairs. Ruth could hear her resounding cough until the doors finally shut behind her.

George stood in the doorway of the drawing room, his face fearful and slightly averted. Ruth took his arm, patted his hand.

'With a bit of luck we shan't see her again,' she said. 'So

you can take that look off your face.' She kissed him, then went back to the kitchen and her cooking.

Dr Weiss returned her lecture notes to their file, plugged in her electric kettle, and made herself a cup of coffee. When her mind had slowly emptied of her conclusion, which, according to habit, she found herself reviewing more critically than when she had delivered it, she opened her mail. This consisted largely of memoranda beginning, 'It has come to my notice that . . . ' or 'It has been brought to my attention that . . . ' Then she reached for a sheet of paper. Dear Ned, she wrote, dear Ned, it is so long since we met and I have six more chapters to show you. I am rather pleased with my study of Diane de Maufrigneuse. Will you come to dinner next week or the week after? It will have to be either Wednesday or Thursday as the weekends are eroded at either end by my father. He is very old now and since my mother's death relies on my company rather heavily. And of course you must be busy yourself. Do let me know when we can meet. P.S. The section on Eugénie Grandet has turned out rather longer than expected. Do you think anyone will notice?